"Don't talk." Christina said as she reached out and touched Miki's lips. Miki almost expected electricity to arc between them.

Miki gently placed her hands on Christina's shoulders. The silk that covered them was exotic, the warmth and softness of her body was intoxicating. She kissed her hair then pulled back. Christina's eyes were feverish, her lips swollen. Miki's desire exploded with no interlude and no moment of exploration. She kissed her hard.

Miki heard the low growl as Christina responded. Their tongues hungry and eager, Miki pulled Christina's hips into hers, and Christina gasped.

Then Christina's mouth was on hers with a yearning that astounded her. Her hands slid up to Miki's cheeks, and she pulled Miki's mouth even closer. Miki felt an insatiable thirst, a craving that at first flamed and then detonated within her. She kissed Christina's eyes, her cheeks, her neck. She slid her hands under Christina's shirt and savored the raw heat she felt against her fingertips.

They kissed again, their tongues seeking each other's sweetness, exploring, pushing the boundaries of boldness. Breathless, she picked Christina up and carried her to the sofa.

Visit

Bella Books

at

BellaBooks.com

or call our toll-free number

1-800-729-4992

Wicked Good Time

DIANA TREMAIN BRAUND

Bella
BOOKS

2005

Bella Books, Inc.
P.O. Box 10543
Tallahassee, FL 32302

First published 1999 by Naiad Press

Printed in the United States of America on acid-free paper
First Edition

Editor: Christi Cassidy
Cover designer: Sandy Knowles

ISBN 1-59493-031-7

About the Author

Diana Tremain Braund continues to live on the coast of Maine in a house that overlooks the water. She and her dog, Bob, who is now six years old, take long walks on the beach. This is where she comes up with ideas for Bella Books.

You can e-mail the author at dtbtiger@yahoo.com.

Chapter One

Miki Jamieson was distracted as she stared out the window. This was definitely going to change her plans for the holiday. Instead of spending Christmas with her friends she would be in Bailey's Cove in Jefferson County, Maine, in a cold cabin trying to solve the problems of a woman she did not know.

A massive gust of wind blew gray clouds of icy sleet up and around the window like a cacophony of tiny iron pellets being dropped on a metal tray, a frigid reminder that it was damn cold out. Her boss was staring at papers as he talked to her about her latest assignment.

"Her name is Christina Reynolds. It appears that she has some tie to the governor. Anyway, he wants us to investigate. Says the local cops have not been as interested in her problem as she thought they should be."

"What's her complaint?"

"Says people have been illegally crossing her land. When she tried to stop them, they started harassing her. You know, noises in the night, tipped-over lawn furniture, mostly kid-type pranks, I would say."

Miki frowned. "Hardly governor stuff. I wonder what the real interest is?"

Colonel John Stevenson raised an eyebrow at the same time he smiled. "I wouldn't be surprised if there was some connection there, either a large donation or influence. He didn't explain, but then, he's the governor and he doesn't have to. I told him I would send you down there. Besides, you should enjoy it. Don't you have family there?"

"My parents live there in the summer. In the winter they're part of that large contingent of snow bunnies who go south." Miki stretched her long legs out in front of her and studied her shoes. "They're in Florida right now."

"You do have a home there?"

"Yes, sir."

"Good, take as much time as you need, but let's get some kind of resolution."

Miki shifted uncomfortably in her seat and saw that the colonel noted the body language.

"You have something to say?"

"No, sir." Miki studied the colonel. He was diminutive in size next to her, but a powerhouse of authority. Word had it that he had wanted to join the Maine State Police after he had graduated from college but was rejected because of his small stature. He became a forest ranger and within 18 years held the top job in the department.

"You do have something to say." he said quietly.

He was watching her. He had told her she was his brightest ranger. She had been promoted fast, not because she was the only woman in the department, he'd said, but because she had strong investigative instincts and a gutsy personality. She was over six feet tall, and her height was intimidating in a world where she dealt mostly with men—hunters, fishermen and a lot of poachers.

"I'm not used to handling this kind of situation, sir. Seems to me this may be a case of hysterics rather than anything else."

The colonel smiled. He took his index finger and scratched inside his ear. "Now if I'd said that, I'd be accused of sexist language."

Miki smiled uncomfortably. "Yes, sir."

"I want you to handle this. I want the governor off my butt, and I want you here. Any questions?"

"No, sir."

Miki played the conversation over and over again in her head as icy sleet turned to swirls of snow. The winter moon was a brilliant gray haze as angry clouds alternately moved in front of the single white light of the night. No stars tonight. They were the missing in action, blinking somewhere, but not here.

She inhaled deeply, the spiny air, razor sharp, squeezing the soft membrane inside her nose. The cold cut at her cheeks, bit at her hands. She threw her packed bag onto the passenger seat and climbed in behind the steering wheel, then eased her quarter-ton green, state issue pickup truck along Route 1.

At the Harrington Truck Stop she pulled in for a stretch break and a sandwich. Back on the road she reached across the dash to push levers into the red zone; her heater hummed full tilt, the windshield kept warm to fend off inside fog. The truck heated rapidly, and Miki drove across slush-covered streets that looked like gray mush squeezed in a cup. The only sound, the rhythmic *rap rap rap* of windshield wipers that turned dots of snow into drops of water. It became hypnotic as she thought about her first night back home. She shook off the drowsiness—remnants of an illusive dream that had encircled her for the last two hours of the trip from Jackman. Following Route 1 along the coast, Miki looked across at the white blanket of snow that stretched like a sensuous nymph to the darkened ocean; the rhythm of the surf sounded like the constant breath of a deep sleep. Scintillating stillness; secure seductress; silent slumber. Winter in Maine.

3

She slowed her truck as she entered Bailey's Cove. Maine's winter, she realized as she looked around at the closed shops on Front Street, kept all but the heartiest indoors on a Friday night. Miki saw a single light coming from one office window and felt relief. Although she had planned to drive straight to her closed cabin, she was pleased to see the office, it was her beacon, her lighthouse. She aimed straight for it and the protection of friendship.

She cracked open the door of Kristan's office. "Go home."

"Mik?" Kristan was out of her chair, almost jumping across her desk to give her a hug.

Miki stood stiff-legged, braced for her friend's unbridled hug. She pulled Kristan against her green uniform jacket and held her tightly, then closed her eyes, happy to be there.

"When, where?" Kristan said as she pulled back, only to grab Miki in another she-bear hug.

"Stop, you sound like—"

"I know, a reporter." Kristan laughed. "This is wonderful. Why didn't you tell me you were coming, you've got to come home with me, you've got to—"

"Stop." Miki held her friend by the arms. "I didn't call because I wasn't sure if I would stop halfway and spend the night. I decided to come straight through, and I was headed for the cabin when I saw your light."

"You're not staying at the cabin tonight or tomorrow night. You haven't been back there in ages. It's going to be cold. Hell, it's going to be freezing, and I refuse to let you stay there." Kristan had her hands on her hips.

"I know better than to argue with that don't-mess-with-me-hands-on-the-hips stance you get when you want to win an argument. But what about—"

"Jennifer? She's fine. She will love seeing you."

"Not in the middle of the night."

"You just wait. Watch." Kristan reached for the telephone and punched in the number. Miki could hear the telephone being picked up on the first ring. Kristan chatted with Jennifer for a few minutes, then looked at Miki. "Have you eaten?"

"Yes, at the truck stop."

"She said yes," Kristan said into the telephone, "But I bet we could persuade her to have a bowl of your beef stew." Kristan listened for a few more seconds, then said, "Yes, love you too," and hung up.

"That's disgusting," Miki said with an understanding smile. "Remind me again, how long have you two been together?"

"Three years, three months and ten days, but it feels like three minutes." Miki liked Kristan's gentle blush. "She wants you to stay; take however long you need. You know we turned the top of the garage into a guesthouse, and she's going over now to turn up the heat."

"I'll stay the night and yes, I will have some of Jennifer's great food, but tomorrow I need to open the cabin. I'm supposed to be hard at work Monday morning."

"So this isn't a vacation?"

"Nope, I've been sent down by the colonel to try and straighten out some weird land-boundary dispute between some Boston woman and the locals. While I'm here I'll also be doing other things, but mostly focusing on that."

"Aha."

"You heard?"

"Uh-huh."

"Has something just happened to the woman who writes?"

"No, Mik, but I'm just glad you're here. We can talk about everything tonight over food. Hang tight while I send this to Bangor."

Kristan pushed the necessary buttons to spell-check her copy, then put the modem in its sending mode to forward the story to Bangor. As the modem dialed the mainframe in Bangor, Kristan reached for the telephone and punched in a number.

She waited. "Hey, little buddy, connect me to the boss." she said.

Hey, Jerry, story is there." She paused. "I doubt you'll have any questions. Pretty cut and dried. Not much more than a manic-depressive going out and scrambling his brain with a three-fifty-seven magnum." Kristan paused, "Okay, but if you need me, call the house." She started shoving things in her desk as she was hanging up the telephone. She reached for her keys to lock the inside door. "Ready?" she said to Miki.

"Is that the assignment editor you wanted to kill last year?"

"Yeah. Weird, we're beginning to like each other. And weirdest of all, I find I like working with him."

"Jennifer has mellowed you, my friend."

Kristan reached for her jacket from the clothes tree behind the door. "You bet, and I love it. Come on, we have a lot to catch up on."

Kristan sat next to Jennifer on the couch, her feet tucked under her, her hair still wet from her shower. Her outstretched fingers touched Jennifer's shoulder. She sipped her glass of wine. "So they sent you down here to deal with the Boston woman," she said to Miki.

"Seems that you know something about it." Miki took a sip of her beer. The heat of the stove was comforting. The lights on the Christmas tree were festive. She smiled to herself. The tree and lights were Jennifer's influence. Before Jennifer, Kristan never gave a thought to decorating touches.

"I don't know much. I've mostly ignored it. Not that it might not someday be a news story. What I've heard is that she moved into her father's camp this fall. Let me correct myself." Kristan held up her wineglass. "Her dad's huge house. Think someone said there's something like five-thousand acres and her house sits in the middle of it. The fight has been over private ownership versus public access."

"She out of bounds?" Jennifer asked.

"I don't know." Kristan scratched her cheek. "There are people who've used that land forever. It has one of the last best bass lakes in the state. And you know bass fishermen. They're more driven than a bull moose during rutting season." She chuckled. "Apparently her grandfather bought it and built the place. Her father used it some, not a lot. So people pretty much had the run of the place."

"Then the daughter moved in," Miki said.

"Yeah. The caretakers that were there quit. Heard they didn't like her. More than likely they didn't like being told what to do. You know how folks around here are. They don't like being ordered about, and certainly not by a woman. After she'd been here for a while she started telling people to stay off her land, and people balked. I know she's complained to the state police and the sheriff's department. So your being here doesn't really surprise me."

"What kinds of complaints?" Jennifer looked at Miki.

"Some minor vandalism," Miki answered. "She also says people been doing weird things at night flashing lights on her windows, making noises around the house." Miki relaxed in her chair. She felt warm and comfortable by the fire. "Sheriff sent one of his deputies to investigate. Deputy said nothing was going on. She called the governor's office. Seems to be a lot of power there. Don't know why, though."

"Ah." Kristan rubbed her thumb against her lips. "Lots of money. Her dad is or was some big mogul in Boston. He had some ties to Maine. I don't know if he contributed a bunch to the Republicans or whatever, but I'm not surprised her call to the governor's office got you here."

"Why you?" Jennifer asked.

"They probably think a woman can deal with an emotional female. You know the drill, the colonel didn't say it, but I suspect he believes she's just a nuisance from away."

"And you?" Jennifer asked.

"Don't know. I haven't even spoken with her yet. I was going to call and tell her I'd been assigned to her case, then decided I'd just go over to her house and talk to her. I can get a better feel watching her eyes. I'm curious about her reaction to my being here."

"Don't expect much. I hear she is one aloof lady." Kristan sipped her wine. "I saw her going into the deeds office a couple of weeks ago. She is really, really beautiful. There is something quite beguiling—" She stopped.

Jennifer raised an eyebrow and looked at Kristan with an expression that was stone serious.

"Not . . . I don't mean . . ." Kristan sputtered.

Miki watched the exchange between her two friends impassively.

"Honest." She held a defensive hand up to Jennifer. "I wasn't looking at her like—"

A barely perceptible smirk tugged at the corners of Jennifer mouth. "You're lucky I know us so well."

Kristan stroked Jennifer's hand. "Thank God," she said softly. "Besides"—she looked sideways at Jennifer— "if I was a betting woman I'd say straight, straight, straight." Kristan dragged out each word.

"You're hardly an expert in that area," Jennifer said wryly. "When we first met"—Jennifer looked at Miki—"she told your friend Jackie I was straight, so you'll need to draw your own conclusion about her judgment in that area."

"But, you have to know my friend here." She nodded toward Miki. "The most beautiful woman could walk into a room and Miki would be oblivious to her looks."

"Really?"

Miki blushed. "I just don't focus on how women look."

"What do you focus on?" Jennifer asked quietly.

"Their warmth. I like kindness and gentleness." Miki stopped. "Their eyes tell me that."

Jennifer tilted her head as if considering what Miki had said.

"Well straight or not"—Miki changed the subject, uncomfortable talking about herself— "I have to figure out what the heck is going on out there. If she's being hassled or is just the paranoid type. I wonder why she's here. The colonel didn't seem to know, just told me to straighten everything out."

"Well, how much of what I've heard is fact and how much is Bailey's Cove soap opera, I don't know. One story says she's running away from a broken affair. Another has her hiding out here because her husband beat her up. Who knows? But I did hear she's here alone." Kristan stopped. "But whatever the hell the reason she's here, I'd hate to think that some of the locals are playing tricks on her. You know, Mik, it wouldn't surprise me. They'd see it as just a little harmless fun."

"I'm surprised that the sheriff hasn't been able to get a handle on this," Miki said, getting up and stretching. She still felt the kinks from the long drive.

"Hey, I love Peter." Kristan jumped to her friend's defense. "But he hates these kinds of disputes. Wants them settled in a civil court and leave his deputies out of it. So I'm not surprised he hasn't put the heart and soul of his department into this."

"And until someone proves something nefarious is going on, it really is just that, a civil case," Jennifer added. "She has the right to post her land. She has the right to keep people off of it."

"But that's the problem." Kristan shook her head. "Won't matter how many no trespassing signs she posts, people will either rip them down or ignore them. I don't envy you your job, Mik. You've got those angry bad bass fishermen who say the hell with rules, and they will harass the hell out of her. Not good."

"That's what I was thinking. Let's hope I can strike some sort of compromise between her and her neighbors." Miki finished her beer. "If I can't I don't know what the governor will do. Probably ship me to someplace like Kittery, where the only investigating I'll do is watching a moose walk through the city." Miki stretched again. "I'm beat."

Kristan had finished her wine, and Jennifer stood up, pulling Kristan by the hand, "I know I have a hungry woman here. I doubt she even stopped for lunch. Let's eat so Miki can get to bed."

Over dinner, the three women talked about mutual friends and their jobs. Miki looked at the clock on the kitchen wall. It was eleven o'clock. "Let me help you with the dishes," she said to Jennifer.

"No way, go. You've had a long drive. Kristan will help."

Miki hugged her friends. "You guys are special. This is a great way to come home."

Chapter Two

Miki spent Sunday opening her camp. She had designed it herself with an open floor plan that created an airy interior, which was cold when she entered. She had not expected to be back during the winter months, so she had shut down the pump and had the electricity turned off.

Fortunately there was wood in the lean-to, so she busied herself with getting the generator started and the water running. By noon there was a fire burning in the wood stove, and the propane water heater was going. She had stopped earlier to pick up kerosene for the lanterns.

It took her two hours to clear snow from the driveway and open the parking area. By late afternoon her snowmobile was unloaded from the back of the truck, and she had gone for a long ride around the boundaries of Christina Reynolds's property wondering if there was an alternate route to the lake. She had lived in the area off and on for most of her life, and like others she had always crossed the Boston people's property to get to the lake. But in those days, no one complained.

Outside the air felt like sandpaper on her face, rough and raw. Her snowmobile suit was her first line of defense against the cold. She noted that there were several manmade paths to the lake, and they ranged over a large area.

Miki drove her snowmobile past the driveway to the house. There were fresh tire tracks in the snow, but the house was set too far in off the road for her to see if the owner was home. Oddly enough, Miki had never been to the house. Kristan's description made it sound like something out of *The Sound of Music*.

Aware that she was trespassing, she backtracked and took one of the established paths down to the lake where several ice fishermen already had their tip-ups set. They were warming themselves around a wood fire, smoking cigarettes and sharing a thermos of coffee.

She stopped to talk with them. Two of the men she knew, Ron Saxon, who owned the Cooper Market, and Jim Moores, a woodsman. She did not know the third man. They introduced him as Billy Clark When she looked at him, he averted his eyes.

When Miki asked them about the Boston woman's efforts to keep people off her property, Ronny and Jimmy cursed, but she knew that was just their testosterone talking, trying to impress her and each other. Billy Clark said nothing.

On Monday morning, Miki parked her truck outside the sheriff's office. She reached for the door handle and stepped out into the cold air. Downtown was robed in Christmas decorations and, for the first time since she had left Jackman, she felt a longing to be home.

Besides seeing the sheriff, she was in town to have her telephone and electricity turned on. She also needed to pick up a few forgotten items at the grocery store. She didn't have to buy too much, she thought. She expected to have the case resolved in two weeks and be back in Aroostook County in time for Christmas.

When Miki stepped inside the sheriff's office, shutting the door on the cold December air, Janey Peabody looked up from her desk. They had gone to school together, and Janey rushed to give Miki a hug before Miki had ever let go of the doorknob.

"You look great." She hugged Miki again.

"So do you."

"I don't know." She frowned. "Even with that heavy jacket on, I can see you're still as lean and trim as when we were in high school." Janey stepped back and patted her stomach and hips. "Two children and just too many sticky buns."

"You look great," Miki assured her. She hugged her again.

"Mik, I am glad you're here." Janey dropped her voice. "I don't like what's been going on. I'm afraid there is going to be some real trouble . . ."

Sheriff Peter Kelley opened the door of his office. "Miki." He offered his hand.

"Peter." Miki did not flinch at the bearlike grip. Peter was much taller than her, but where Miki's stomach was flat, Peter's pushed hard against his shirt. He also had developed a dramatic pate that he tried to hide with long strands of hair.

"When did you get in?"

"Friday night. Got my camp open. I'm pretty well settled."

"Wife and I will have to have you over for dinner. I told her you were back here, going to solve all our problems." Miki detected the acerbic tone in his voice.

"Not all of your problems," she kidded. "I'm not even sure I can solve this one."

"Well, if you don't, you can bet that woman will be on the telephone to the governor. You'll be lucky if you still have a job when she gets through with you."

Miki knew Peter had probably gone off like a volcano when he had heard the governor had intervened and called in the "staties." Miki was a statie. Cops in Maine were jealously jurisdictional, and she'd be walking on eggs in this case, hoping to find a solution without pissing off the locals.

13

"Come in. I told Scott Forrest to be here at nine a.m."

Miki glanced up at the clock. She had about three minutes.

"He's the young fella I put on the case. He's had his hands full with her, but I know he's done a good job," Peter said defensively. "He tried to talk with her, been real gentle, but she's just disagreeable. Claims people been harassing her, tearing down no trespassing signs. Personally, I think it's kids. She also claims someone has been around her house at night trying to spook her. But I'll let him tell ya. How about some coffee. Janey, get Mik some coffee." Peter acknowledged his secretary for the first time.

"No, thanks. I had breakfast at Tippy's this morning, and I'm afloat with coffee." Miki had unbuttoned her coat when she entered the office. But now she started to take it off. "Okay if I leave this here?" she asked Janey.

"Sure, hon, throw it over the chair there."

"One thing I do remember is that your secretary here used to make the best cinnamon buns in the world. I hope I can have one of those."

Janey beamed. "That's where all this weight comes from. I didn't bring in any today. But you stop by the house sometime this week and I'll get you a whole armful."

"I'll do that." Miki heard the outside door open and saw a deputy enter the hallway and close the door.

"Here's Scott now." The sheriff nodded at the glass that separated the inside door from the hallway. Miki watched as the man stamped snow off his feet. She figured he had about four inches on her and was a lot younger, probably in his early 30s. He had that cocky confidence some cops exude from their pores.

He turned to the door and saw her watching him. She knew he was sizing her up. He was good looking, Miki decided, if you liked that kind of masculine look. High cheekbones, crisp military haircut, full lips and a black thinly trimmed mustache were his most distinguishing features. Miki sensed an instant dislike. He kept watching her as he opened the interior door to the office.

"Scott, this is Miki Jamieson, Maine Forest Ranger. I told you

14

the state boys sent her down here to give you a hand in sorting out the dispute with that Reynolds woman."

The deputy smiled at Miki and took her hand. It wasn't the firm grip she had received just minutes before from the sheriff. It was a lingering sensual hold. Nope, she decided. She really did not like this make-believe stud.

"She won't listen to reason. Tried to talk to her." Scott had glistening white teeth to go with the full lips. His baritone voice struck Miki as a cultivated affectation.

"Scott's my best man. I figured if anyone could persuade her to back off, he could do it, but let's go into my office. Janey, bring Scott and me some coffee would ya."

Seated opposite the sheriff, Miki turned her chair so she could observe Scott as they spoke. He was seated comfortably next to her, his right leg over his left. His militarily creased deputy's uniform was spotless.

"When did you begin your investigation?" Miki stopped as Janey opened the door, carrying the two coffees. She set one in front of the sheriff and handed the other to Scott, then winked at Miki as she quietly closed the door behind her.

Scott took a sip of his coffee and then set the cup on the sheriff's worn pine desk. He pulled a small spiral notebook from his inside jacket pocket. "First time was about a month ago. Said people were crossing over her land with snowmobiles and three-wheelers. Said some were even going up her driveway, right next to her house. Then"—Scott turned the pages on his notebook— "she called four times after that, same complaint. About a week or two after Thanksgiving she called to say she heard noises outside the house."

"What kind of noises?"

"Said it sounded like rocks being tossed on the roof. I expect a raccoon been up there—she's got trees all around her house, so I expect that's mostly what it was."

15

"Did you get up on a ladder and investigate?"

"Naw, we'd just had snow, so there was no point climbing around on her roof looking for raccoon prints." Scott looked at his notes. "She complained two more times after that someone had been on her property during the night. Flashing lights, again throwing things on her roof. Each time we come up empty-handed."

"Of course if you'd climbed around on her roof, you might have found pebbles, rocks, some kind of debris that would make that noise, if in fact someone was harassing her," Miki countered.

Scott shifted in his seat. "Look, I think we just have a hysterical woman here, although"—Scott shifted again and tugged at the creases on his pants—"she is a beauty." He stopped and swallowed clearly replaying his fantasies. She was glad she didn't have a view of those images. She made a mental bet with herself that the woman had rejected Scott's effort to charm her and that he had written off her complaints.

"Course, that's not what's important here," the sheriff interceded.

"No, it isn't," Miki added softly.

"Well, I've got an appreciative eye." Scott bristled.

"Have you set up any kind of surveillance, to see if anyone is harassing her at night?" Miki ignored Scott and directed her question to the sheriff.

"Don't have the manpower," Peter answered too quickly.

Miki watched as the sheriff's eyes shifted from her face. She could tell he was lying. If a local had a similar complaint, he'd find the manpower to put an end to it. She had little doubt that someone was harassing the woman. "Anything else?" she asked.

"Yeah, she has an unlisted telephone, but she says it rings and when she picks it up she can hear someone breathing." Scott smirked.

"Well, if it's unlisted how did a breather get the number?"

"Don't know. I think it's a misdial and she's just imagining the breathing part."

"So according to your estimate, the woman's doing a lot of imagining." Miki tossed back at him.

He closed his notebook, stuck it back in his inside jacket pocket. "That's how I'd size it up. Or maybe kids into pranks. It happens and usually ends as quick as it starts."

"Is she alone there?"

"I think, maybe," the sheriff answered. "Heard she was married, although I don't think he's been up here. No kids, at least with her. Maybe some kind of domestic thing. Look, Miki, this is a tough one. People have been using that land for years. Her old man never said a word."

"He wasn't around here much," Miki said.

"True, but I think men understand these things better than women. Look, if no one's doing anything more than just crossing her land to get to some of the best damn bass fishing in Maine, what's the complaint?" Miki sensed that the sheriff had used that argument before.

"Sounds as though it might be more than just that."

"Then that's her fault. She put up those no trespassing signs. You know that's like dumping a school of herring in front of a shark. People are going to react, and they did. They've never had to deal with no trespassing signs before, so they tore them down. I can understand that. It takes time for folks to adjust." The sheriff was unbending.

"Have you spoken with her, Peter?"

"Just when she came into the office to make her first complaint. After that I let Scott handle it. He's my best man," the sheriff said again. Miki hid the internal shudder coursing through her body.

"Anything else?" Miki watched the flicker of nonverbal communication between the two men.

"Well." Scott hesitated.

"I need it all, gentlemen." Miki tried to keep the impatience out of her voice.

"Well. Just that she claims someone tried to break in."

"When?"

"Day before yesterday."

"Did you investigate?"

"Yeah, but again . . ." Scott shrugged. "There was nothing to prove anyone even tried."

"Any evidence?"

"Some scratch marks around a living room window where she said she heard noise, but they could have been there for some time."

"What kind of scratch marks?"

"You know, what a screwdriver would make if someone was trying to pry off a storm window." Scott was clearly not enjoying this line of questioning.

"Fresh scratch marks are quite different from old ones."

Scott shifted impatiently in his seat. "I looked at them, and again I think we just got a beautiful woman who is a hysteric because she doesn't want to be alone. Probably be better off if she had a man out there with her."

Miki suppressed a smile. She wondered at how unpleasant the woman had been when she rejected Scott's advances. She bet she had done a number on him.

"You going out there?" the deputy asked.

"Soon. I have a few stops to make in town."

"Well, don't expect friendly treatment."

Miki nodded noncommittally.

"If you need any help," Peter said, "you just give us a call. Like I said, Scott's my best man and I'll—"

"That won't be necessary, sheriff," Miki cut him off. "Right now I want to see if we can start from the beginning and reach some kind of compromise."

"That's going to be difficult. That's one of the things I directed Scott to try and do." He looked at the young deputy who remained seated, staring at his nails. "And she wouldn't even talk with him about it."

Miki looked down at Scott. No Henry Kissinger, he probably

18

never thought of trying to reach a rapprochement between the woman and the locals.

"Don't bother, sheriff. You don't have to see me out. I know my way." Miki shook his hand. She ignored Scott.

Janey had her back to her, her face focused on the computer screen. She glanced back and saw the sheriff and deputy talking. Given the expression on Scott's face she suspected she was the topic and their assessment was not very flattering. She had dealt with the Scotts of the world ever since her first days at the police academy, and she had heard them all. "Lesbo," "queer," "ball-breaker." Most men didn't stop there. Her size intimidated them, so there were also the usual "moose," "Amazon," "shark," "bull-dog" assessments.

"Janey," Miki said softly. She turned in her chair.

"Sorry, Miki, I thought it was the sheriff. I just ignore him most of the time, let him get his own coffee."

"I'd like to talk to you." Miki kept her back to the door, blocking the sheriff's view of her conversation with his secretary. "But not here. Okay if I stop by your house some night this week?"

"Absolutely, and I promise to have some cinnamon sticky buns waiting for you when you get there. Just call and let me know what night."

Miki picked up her coat. "That's enough of a temptation even without the questions." She smiled.

"Good to see you, Mik. I'm so glad you're on this one."

"Well, I don't know if I'm glad about the case, but it's nice to be home again."

Chapter Three

Miki parked about halfway down the driveway. She wanted to walk the rest of the way to get a feel for where the house was in relationship to the rest of the property and the lake, so she could decide where to set up her surveillance.

She stopped to listen to the chickadees. There must have been hundreds hiding inside the boughs of the spruce trees that lined the driveway. Fragile, yet flirtatious with humans, they most often were seen in winter, their black, gray and white feathers shielding them from the cold. You didn't need a mood tape with them around.

A white rabbit peeked out from under some brush. Its pink nose twittered when it saw Miki, and then the rabbit scurried across the driveway.

She looked overhead and drew a deep breath. Summers would be beautiful here, she thought. The maple trees among the pines would provide a wonderful canopy of protection, like the entrance of a cave. Now the sun that cut through the leafless trees provided a pattern of shadows on the ground.

She stopped as the house came into view. The size was overwhelming. The house was natural cedar with four peaks. Dormers with large picture windows dominated the second floor. No doubt there were some really large bedrooms up there, Miki thought. There was a large wraparound porch that commanded attention at the front of the house. The afternoon sun reflecting on the windows created a red haze that made the windows look as though they were on fire. Impressive, Miki thought, isolated and impressive.

Beside the house, there was a woman on her knees. Her knit ski cap was pushed back on her head, and strands of black hair hung loosely around her face. From a distance, Miki tried to figure out what she was doing.

She kicked herself for leaving her truck parked back on the driveway. If anything she might scare her. She decided to cut through the trees. She knew the racket would direct the woman's attention to the noise. She hoped she didn't have a gun.

Pushing through the snow-covered limbs, she was startled when some snow dumped down her neck. She had pulled her coat collar up, but it had only served to provide a scoop that caught the snow and poured it down her collar, where it melted and ran down her back. *Serves you right*, she thought. *You'll be soaked by the time you reach her.*

As Miki cleared the last stand of trees, she saw the woman looking in her direction, shading her eyes with her hand.

"Mrs. Reynolds," she called out. "My name's Miki Jamieson, with the Maine Forest Service." She headed toward the woman, lowering her voice as she got closer.

"Your car break down?"

"No." Miki stood looking down at her. Kristan was right, Miki thought. The woman is beautiful. "Actually, now that I rethink this walk, I really don't have a very good reason why I did it." Miki could feel a blush creeping up her cheeks to blend with the cold red already there.

"You're lucky I didn't have a gun."

"I'd say," Miki said nodding in agreement. She held out her hand. "Miki Jamieson. As I said, I'm with the Maine Forest Service. I've been asked to investigate the problems you've been having."

Christina pulled off her glove. Her hand was warm as Miki shook it. "So the governor sent a woman. Interesting."

"The governor sent an investigator to look into your complaints," Miki countered.

"Touché."

Miki felt a slight discomfort as Christina studied first her face and then her height. Miki looked down at the bird feeder lying on the snow.

Christina followed her gaze. "The wire came off the top and I was trying to fix it, but I'm afraid I'm not very handy."

Miki pushed her ranger cap back on her head and knelt in the snow. One of the two eyelets that secured the bird feeder to a wire had pulled loose and the other one was bent. "Mind if I help?"

"Please."

"Do you have a pair of pliers?"

"I have what's in that box there. I found it in the shed."

Miki dug around in the small red toolbox and pulled out a pair of needle-nose pliers. She straightened the bent eyelet. Then she removed the wire from each of the eyelets, picked up the bird feeder and brushed the snow off of the roof. She screwed the loose eyelet into the front of the feeder and restrung the wire between them, twisting the end of the wire to close the loop. "Where would you like to hang this?"

"Over there. I'd like it as high up into the tree as possible, but not so high that I can't reach it to fill it every day."

Miki guessed that Christina was about six inches shorter than she was. "You should be able to reach that quite comfortably," she said as she hung the feeder.

Christina smiled approvingly for the first time. "Thank you, Ranger. Can I offer you some coffee?"

22

"Thanks." Miki followed her through a back door and into a mud room, where Christina pulled off her hat and jacket, then took a comb out of her hair. Long black curly hair fell to her shoulders.

"Can I take your coat?"

"No, thanks, I'm fine."

"Ah. This is not going to be a social visit."

Miki trailed Christina into a massive kitchen, which reminded her of the one at the police academy. Large copper pots hung on a wire rack above the cooktop. There were two double-wide refrigerators, two ovens and three microwaves, stainless steel sinks and worktables. Everything seemed to be a circle around the center island. Miki blinked. Her entire camp would fit inside this kitchen.

"Monstrous, isn't it." Christina smiled. Miki liked the smile, it was a far cry from the cold appraising look Christina had given her while she was fixing the bird feeder.

"I'd say."

"You can't imagine how silly you feel in here when all you want to do is make a sandwich. By the time you walk around the kitchen you almost forget why you're there." She smiled again. "My grandfather used to do a lot of entertaining here. Big parties, lots of guests from Boston. My father and mother did some of that early on, but Mother never really liked the place so they didn't come here very much, which I think is part of the problem. You see, Ranger—"

"Miki."

"You see, Miki, I understand what all the discourse is about, but I can't change the fact that I own all of this and I want my privacy. I don't think it's too much to ask people to just leave me alone."

"It's a little more difficult than that, but why don't we start from the beginning. I'd like you to tell me how it all started."

"Didn't that sheriff's deputy tell you? He's certainly been here enough."

Miki heard the cynical tone. It confirmed her belief that Scott had displayed more than a professional interest and that Christina had not welcomed his attentions.

23

"Why don't we just start from the beginning."

"Of course. Let me get you some coffee." Christina turned toward the stove. "Would you like to sit in here, or would you prefer we took the coffee into the atrium?"

"Here's fine," Miki said unbuttoning her jacket. She reached to her inside pocket and pulled out a notebook.

"Sit down." Christina gestured toward a giant oak table with large oak chairs surrounding it. "Are you from around here?"

"At one time."

"Where do you live now?"

"Jackman."

Christina poured coffee into two large mugs. "Wow, that's really north."

"A bit." Miki smiled for the first time. Scott was right, Miki thought. Christina's figure was model perfect, and the blue silk blouse only accented it. The blouse dipped down to a thin waist and was tucked neatly in dark blue slacks. Christina's eyes were black, and her face reminded Miki of Nefertiti's. High cheekbones, small mouth with full lips, a long neck.

Christina set the pot down. "Sugar, cream?"

"Just black, thanks."

Christina reached into one of the refrigerators near the table, pulled out a pitcher and added cream to her cup. "Are you always this talkative?"

Miki smiled. "Mrs. Reynolds—"

"Christina. Mrs. Reynolds sounds a bit too formal."

"Christina, I'm here to investigate your complaint."

"Don't they teach you social skills at the police academy. That's where you went to school, right?"

"Yes."

"Yes, that's where you went to school, or yes, they taught social skills?"

Miki shook her head and smiled. "Mrs. Reynolds, I think you're pulling my leg just a wee bit."

"Just a bit." Christina smiled. She set a cup in front of Miki and pulled out a chair opposite her.

"Ask your questions, Ranger."

"How long have you been here?"

"I arrived just before Thanksgiving"—Christina paused as she framed her answer—"I wanted some time alone." She sipped her coffee.

"No family here?"

"My husband is in Boston. He is . . . busy. My father . . . recently passed away."

"I'm sorry," Miki said, noting there was no wedding band on Christina's hand.

"So am I, Ranger. So am I."

For the next hour Miki questioned Christina about the problems she had encountered. Much she had already learned from Scott. Factually, Christina's account did not vary.

She studied Christina as she recounted dates and times of each occurrence. Although she had not asked her age, Miki guessed that she was around forty. She liked her voice. It was smooth and soft like fine-woven silk.

"You're not taking very many notes." Christina's expression was teasing.

"Actually, I've looked at the police reports."

"Has this been some kind of test? To see if I could remember what I told the deputy?"

"No, actually, I was looking for a variation. To see if you might remember something more than what you told the deputy."

"I don't think I do. Unfortunately, whoever is doing this is doing it at night, usually after I've been asleep for hours."

"Is there any kind of pattern?"

"Pattern?"

"Yes, does it happen at certain times? Every Tuesday, something like that."

"No, it's pretty random. It's happened at midnight and sometimes at four in the morning, not every night, sometimes not every week."

"Are you afraid?"

"More angry than scared."

"Do you have a weapon in the house?"

"Other than the knives in the kitchen, no. I wouldn't know how to use a gun if I had one." Christina looked down at the bulge in Miki's jacket. "I take it you do know how to use a gun."

"Yes."

"Have you ever shot anyone?"

Miki grinned. "That's only on television. In real life forest rangers rarely do any shooting."

Christina looked down at her coffee. When she raised her face again, Miki saw the worry in her eyes.

"So do you agree with the young deputy, that I'm just a loony who needs a man around to protect her?"

"No."

"Thank you." Christina leaned back in her chair for the first time since the conversation began. She smiled, and Miki watched Christina's face relax. "I was just going to make myself something to eat. Would you like a sandwich?"

"No, thanks, I have to go." Miki closed her notebook and tucked it in her inside pocket.

"So what's next?"

"I catch the people who are doing this to you."

"Just like that."

"Hopefully." Miki scratched the back of her neck. "Mrs. Reynolds, I'm going to need to set up some kind of surveillance. About the only consistency I've gleaned from what you've told me is that most of the noises occur at night."

"What do you mean by a surveillance?"

"I'll spend some nights here on your property. Random nights. Hopefully, I pick a night when the perpetrator decides to bother you. "

"At the house?"

"Actually, out in the woods."

"Won't you freeze to death?"

"No, I'll be fine." Miki smiled.

Christina frowned.

"Really, I'll be fine." Miki leaned forward. Hands cradling the cup. "As I said, that hopefully will solve that problem. The problem of access will be something else again. People around here have been crossing your property for years."

Christina looked at a spot over Miki's head. "I know." Miki waited for Christina to continue. "When do you expect to do this surveillance thing?"

"I thought I might begin tonight. I'd appreciate it if you wouldn't mention that to anyone."

"Not to worry, Ranger. I live the monastic life here. I rarely see anyone to speak with."

Miki stood up. "Thank you for the coffee."

"Would you like a ride down to your car?"

Miki felt the heat climbing up her neck. "No, thanks, I can walk."

Christina's eyes were critical in their appraisal. "Just out of curiosity, what did you expect to find?"

"I honestly don't know."

Chapter Four

Miki set her alarm for eleven p.m. She rolled over when it rang and slapped at the button. The wood stove had burned down, and she really wanted to cuddle under her down comforter for a few more minutes, but she pushed back the covers and reluctantly hauled herself out of bed.

She went into the bathroom, brushed her teeth and ran a hand through her straight, in-between color hair, not quite blond, not quite brown. She knew it was going to be a long night, but her snowmobile suit would keep out the cold. She planned to snowmobile over, cutting through the wooded area even though it would take longer. If she used her state truck with the agency's emblem on the side, it would be a neon sign advertising the surveillance. There were no secrets in this small community.

Miki thought about Christina warm in her bed. Her first impression had been good. She liked her. Although she could sense the woman's uneasiness while she was questioned, she had reacted right. She reminded Miki of a willow tree, easily bent, vulnerable. You wanted to protect her. She suspected Christina brought out that quality in most people.

She poured coffee into her thermos, stuck a couple of sandwiches into her backpack and headed out the door. The cold stopped her in her tracks. The radio report said temperatures were going to drop during the night, but she was unprepared for the biting wind. The sting on her face told her the wind chill must be somewhere around forty below. She had a full-face ski mask tucked in one of the compartments on her snowmobile. She pulled it out, pulled her hood back and put it on. Then she snapped the straps to her hood under her chin.

Miki followed the paths the deer and smaller animals had made in the snow. It took her about twenty minutes to get to the stand of trees she had picked out earlier. She turned out the headlight on her snowmobile and parked it there. She would have to walk the rest of the way in so the noise of the machine wouldn't scare anyone off.

Although most cops hated surveillance, Miki enjoyed it. She spent the quiet time thinking about the principals in the case—Christina, Scott and even Peter. She wished Peter hadn't been so intractable. Ordinarily when she came into another cop's jurisdiction, she would brief him on her plans. This time she decided a closed-mouth approach was best.

Clouds obliterated the moon, which made it easier to stay in the shadow of the trees but also made walking more difficult. Without moonlight or a flashlight, she had to pick her way over broken limbs and through thick brush.

She found a good spot just to the left of the house. She placed a small plastic tarp on the ground and then sat down and opened her thermos. She was on her third cup of coffee when she heard the crack of a twig. She set her coffee on the ground and stood up.

"I can smell your coffee." The voice came from just behind her. Christina must have left her house by the back door and circled around.

"Mrs. Reynolds?" Miki couldn't keep the impatience out of her voice.

"Christina," she answered softly.

"Mrs. Reynolds, what are you doing out here?"

"I thought you'd like some coffee," she said matter-of-factly. Within minutes she was a dark silhouette against the trees as she walked toward Miki.

"Ah. Mrs. Reynolds, this won't do. If anyone was around here our voices would have scared them off."

"No one is going to be out on a night like this, not even someone trying to scare me."

"Well, I'm crazy enough to be out here." Miki was irritated. She pulled up her ski mask so she would look less menacing.

"And now you're upset with me. I'm sorry," Christina whispered. She handed the mug of coffee to Miki. "I really was just trying to help."

"Thank you." She took the cup. She realized she would win few arguments with this woman.

"I was thinking. I have a shed over there. It would make more sense for you to stand in there. There's a window, and you'd be out of the wind."

Miki looked over Christina's head at the building next to the house. "That could work, but I'm set up here, so I might as well stay for another hour or so."

"When are you going to do this again?"

Miki smiled in spite of her irritation. "I don't think I'll tell you. Surveillance doesn't mean two people standing out in the cold talking. It means my being out here alone watching."

"I realize that, Ranger, but I was thinking, if you're going to use the shed, I'd leave it unlocked."

"I'll use the shed." Miki gave in. "Now, why don't you go back to the house. And leave me to my job."

"Very well. Don't worry about the cup."

Miki stayed out another hour, but had to agree with Christina that no one would be out on such a cold night. She returned to her cabin and slept most of the morning, then went into town to get more supplies. She purposely avoided the sheriff. She tried Kristan's office, but the door was locked.

About five p.m. she stopped at Janey's house. She had called her earlier and they had agreed to meet.

The small warm kitchen stood in stark contrast with Christina's, which had an almost institutional feel to it. Janey's two young children were at the kitchen table helping their mother.

"Just in time." Janey turned to her stovetop and lifted a plate of sticky buns from the warming tray.

"Ohhhh," Miki groaned. "They look wonderful. I haven't had fresh bakery since the last time I visited you."

"Well, there's enough here for you to take home." Janey smiled. Miki unbuttoned her jacket and threw it across a chair and sat down.

"Yeah, we had to wait until you got here," Mark said, eyeing the platter. "Mom said we could have one."

Miki reached over and tousled the nine-year-old's hair. "Well, I'm sorry you had to wait. How about we dig in."

"Yeah," six-year-old Kimberly agreed. She scrambled off her chair and onto Miki's lap. "I want to eat with you."

"Get down and don't bother Miki," Janey scolded.

"She's okay."

"They're a handful, I'll tell you." Janey turned toward the refrigerator. "Coffee? Milk?"

"Milk," the youngsters said in unison.

"Manners!" Janey frowned at them. "I am talking to Miki."

"Coffee would be great."

Miki watched Janey as she moved around the kitchen. She placed a sticky bun on each plate and poured two large glasses of milk. "Come on, you two, Miki and I want to talk. Go watch some television."

"What you going to talk about?" Kimberly looked at Miki. Her eyes were as green as her mother's. Her straight blond hair was cut like a cap on her head.

31

"Big people stuff." Mark said matter-of-factly. "Stuff they don't want us to hear. Come on." He took his sister's hand and followed their mother into the other room. Miki could hear the television.

"I'm glad you stopped by," Janey said when she came back to the kitchen. She set out plates and two cups of hot steaming coffee, then passed the plate of sticky buns to Miki. "Eat. You're too skinny."

"I'm not too skinny."

"Yes, you are."

Miki laughed, comfortable in her old friend's kitchen. "So what's going on, Janey?"

"You know I don't usually talk about things at the sheriff's office, but I don't like this, Miki. I wanted you to know there's something weird going on."

"What?" Miki bit into the still warm sticky bun and groaned. "This is great. Sinfully wonderful," she said with a full mouth.

"Thank you." Janey beamed. She bit into her own sticky bun and nodded approvingly. She put it down on her plate and licked her fingers. "I feel sorry for that woman. I've talked to her a couple of times when she called to report another incident. I believe her, Miki. I think she is being harassed, and I think Scott's giving her the shoofly routine."

"Shoofly?"

"Ya know, soothing words and then blowing her off. Plus, I got to tell you I heard him talking with her. He's been giving her the come-on. It's getting way too . . ."

"Personal?"

"Yeah." Janey sipped at her coffee. "It's not right. She not only has to worry about who's been harassing her, she has that jerk to think about."

"Did she complain to the sheriff?"

"Yeah, but it doesn't get her anywhere. Scott's got him by the short hairs. He thinks the world of Scott, and that deputy trades on it. I don't like it."

"So you believe she's being harassed?"

"Absolutely, and I think Scott knows it too. It's hard to describe, but once when I was coming back from lunch I heard him on the telephone. His back was to the door so he didn't see me come in. When he saw me he got up real fast. Then quizzed me to see if I'd heard anything. I guess I had, but you know how you don't pay attention."

"Can you remember anything at all?"

"I've racked my brain, but nothing. I just wasn't paying attention. I only got suspicious after he started asking me about what I heard." Miki sipped at her coffee, and Janey held out the plate. "Have another sticky bun."

"I can't. I've had two. One more and I'm not going to want to go home. Just curl up in front of that wood stove and sleep."

Janey laughed. "Miki, I'm so glad you're here. Mrs. Reynolds is good people, and I know you'll be able to help her."

"Let's hope. You see anyone different hanging around the sheriff's office lately, talking with Scott?"

"Just the regulars. Nothing out of the ordinary."

Miki and Janey visited for another hour, reminiscing about their high school days. Janey wouldn't let Miki leave until she had extracted a promise that she would go to mass at St. James Catholic Church on Christmas Eve.

Janey, over Miki's polite but mild protests, wrapped up several sticky buns and popped them in a bag for her to take home.

Miki checked the time on the clock in her truck. She would sleep for a few hours and then head back to Christina's.

At ten p.m. Miki got up and made her way to Christina's, again staying on the back trail. She parked her snowmobile in the stand of trees and crept to the shed. When she opened the door, the warmth assaulted her face. She could see the red blow of a space heater that had been turned so that the light faced a wall.

Using a penlight cupped in her hand, Miki looked around the shed. A pot of coffee was on the table, a chair nearby.

For the rest of the week she established a routine of setting her alarm to get up in the middle of the night. After the first night, sandwiches appeared along with the coffee. At least, Miki thought, she made surveillance a comfortable experience. But Miki was also frustrated. After a week and a lot of lost sleep, she still had no clue about who was bothering the woman.

Chapter Five

Jennifer had invited Miki to spend Christmas Eve and Christmas Day with her and Kristan at her parents' house in Portland, but Miki declined, worried that it would put her too far away if something happened at Christina's. Their friend Jackie, who grew up with her and Kristan, had gone off with friends to Florida. She and Miki had spoken on the phone several times and had promised to get together for dinner after the holidays.

She frowned at her watch; it was seven-thirty p.m. Janey had called that day and reminded her of her promise to go to evening services. Janey sang in the choir, and she wanted Miki there.

Well, she thought. Christmas alone, that's a first. She really wanted to stay at the cabin and feel sorry for herself, but she knew that eventually she would have to face Janey.

A few minutes before eight she got in her truck and drove the short distance to the church. Cars lined both sides of the street, and Miki had to park a distance away. She could hear the organ music before she opened the door. Mark handed her a program as she entered and whispered that his mother was downstairs.

"Where's your sister?" Miki asked.

"Downstairs with Mom." Miki was going to ask him another question, but other people were behind her waiting for their programs.

The church was packed, but she saw an empty seat in the middle of the last pew and hoped the early arrivers would move rather than make her step between their feet and the kneeling rail.

She stood beside the pew, and it reminded Miki of a gray wave when the elderly women who were seated there looked to their left, then one after the other moved over to leave her the aisle seat.

Miki studied her program. Aha, she thought. No wonder Janey had been so insistent she be there. She was going to sing a solo.

Miki unzipped her jacket and in the small space of the pew eased it off. It was when she leaned forward to reach for a hymnal that she saw Christina two pews in front of her. She looked elegant, her black hair pulled back into a chignon. She had often wondered how women had the patience to style their hair that way. The red and blue Christmas lights made her gold dangling earrings glitter. Miki could only see her shoulders and her velvety green top. She wondered if it reached down to became a dress or was a blouse tucked into a skirt. Somehow she knew Christina would not be wearing pants.

Her attention was drawn to the front of the church as the organ began to play. Out of the corner of her eyes she saw the choir lined up behind her. The procession reached deep into the vestibule. She had been so fixed on Christina she had not heard what was going on just a few feet behind her.

The choir, with hymnals open, marched past Miki. She felt a hand on her shoulder and a slight squeeze and looked up at Janey's smiling face. Janey did not miss a beat as she sang *O Come, All Ye Faithful* with the choir as it marched to the side of the altar. Miki felt warmed by the touch. Even in high school, Janey had a mothering quality that made you feel a part of her life.

For the rest of the evening, Miki followed the service, kneeling or standing when appropriate, and watching Christina. She realized she was watching Christina more than she was the priest. Even the sermon on purity of deed seemed to drop into the background. Miki looked down at the program. Janey's solo was next.

As the organ began to play, Miki closed her eyes to the first few notes of the *Ave Maria*, then Janey's crystalline soprano voice filled the church. She had heard Janey sing in high school, but maturity had flawlessly polished her voice. She listened to the haunting melody, and although the Latin was lost on her, the emotional impact needed no interpretation. Christina, she saw, was wiping tears from her eyes.

As Janey's voice reached to the highest notes, the choir joined in, and the melding of voices made Miki shiver. All eyes were on Janey as the hymn came to an end. Miki realized that the entire congregation had been holding its breath. After a few moments of silence, the bells in the church tower began to ring.

The priest stepped forward. "May the peace of the Lord be with you. And will you share in that peace by offering your hand to your neighbor." Miki turned to her left to shake the hands of the women next to her. She watched as Christina shook hands with people in front of her and then turned around to shake hands with those seated behind her. Christina smiled in recognition when she saw Miki. She smiled and reached forward.

Miki leaned across the pew in front of her and took her hand. "Peace," she said quietly to Christina.

"And peace to you."

Miki felt overwhelmed by the exotic radiance of her eyes as dark as onyx. She swallowed, smiled, realized she was still holding her hand and let go. Communion was a jumble as Miki tried to focus.

Reality returned when the recessional began, and Janey touched her hand as she walked down the aisle with the choir singing *Joy to the World*. Miki picked up her jacket and stepped aside to let the other people in her pew leave while she waited for Christina.

"Good evening, Ranger." Christina smiled up at Miki.

"Mrs. Reynolds." Miki smiled back. "Would you like . . ."

"Oh, there you are," Janey said, still garbed in her white robe. She hugged Miki and then Christina. "I'm so glad you could come."

"I'm so glad I did. You have a magnificent voice," Christina said softly.

Miki saw the shyness in Janey's eyes. "Thank you."

"Janey, it was beautiful. I remember that voice from high school, but wow."

Janey laughed, clearly embarrassed at the attention. "You have to come to the house."

"I—" Miki started.

"Miki Jamieson, don't argue. You bring Christina. There's just going to be a few of us. Just a little Christmas get-together. You can have some mulled cider, and I promise to send you home with an armful of cinnamon buns."

Miki looked at Christina.

"Who could resist such an invitation?" Christina asked.

"I don't think she'll let us."

"That's right. Christina, you can ride with Miki because it's crazy getting to my house. She can bring you back to your car later," Janey said as she turned to another couple who was standing nearby.

Miki gestured for Christina to go ahead of her. "Look," she said as they stood outside on the church steps. "If you'd prefer to follow me over in your car, that's fine."

"I don't think I'd better. Janey was pretty exact about how we should do it." Christina raised her eyebrow as she looked up at Miki. "I bet you never win an argument with her."

"Hardly ever." Miki laughed. "How do you know her?"

"Just over the telephone when I called to report the problems at the house. After two or three calls, I felt like I had been talking to someone I knew my whole life. I suspect she gets that reaction from everyone."

"She does. Even in high school, Janey never knew a stranger.

She has this giant wing, and everyone ends up under it at one time or another."

When they reached her truck, Miki opened the passenger door. She looked down at Christina's dress and high heels. "I think I'd better give you a hand up. This truck has a pretty high carriage."

"Thank you." Christina reached out her hand, and Miki easily balanced the weight of her arm as she stepped up onto the running board and then into the cab. Miki marveled at how gracefully she executed the move.

Miki walked around to her side and seated herself behind the wheel. "Did Janey invite you to Mass?"

"As a matter of fact, she did. I was going to curl up with a good book and pretend tonight was just another night of the year. Now I'm glad she insisted that I come. She has an unforgettable voice."

"She was in our high school glee club, and I always knew she could sing, but tonight . . ."

"Yes, it was unbelievably special." Miki wondered if Christina's tears had been because of the emotion of the music or something deeper.

They rode along in companionable silence. Miki turned off of Route 1, and went down a woods road. The houses they passed were spaced acres apart, but all were decorated with Christmas lights on trees and bushes and around windows. One house had a spotlight trained on its chimney where a plastic Santa Claus stood nearby ready to climb down.

"I thought maybe you'd head to Boston for the holidays."

"I had planned to, but I didn't feel up to the challenge of this unpredictable weather, and I really didn't want to get stuck down there." Miki waited for Christina to say more, but the woman was silent. "How about you? Where would you be tonight if you hadn't had to baby-sit me?"

"Well, I'm not exactly baby-sitting you." Miki laughed. "I'd be with friends in Jackman. We get together every Christmas."

"I'm sorry. I should have gone to Boston, then you could at least have been somewhere that you wanted to be tonight."

"This is fine," Miki said, and she really meant it.

"Did you plan to do that surveillance thing tonight?"

"I had planned on it. In fact, I was going to go to your house after the church service."

"Well, this is much nicer."

"I agree." Miki said as she pulled into the driveway.

Christina looked at the empty house. "Looks like we're going to have to wait."

"Come on." Miki helped Christina down.

"Are we going to break in?"

"Nope, we're going to walk in." Miki reached for the doorknob and turned it. She could smell the food even before she was inside. "Nobody locks a door around here."

"Are you serious?"

"Dead serious."

The kitchen table was filled with food and Miki could smell the mulled cider.

"Let me take your coat," Miki offered. Cars rumbled outside. "I expect that's Janey and her family now. Have you met her husband?"

"No."

"Well, he's not at all like her. Where Janey is a fountain, he's a desert. Quiet as all get out. Nice as can be, but mostly stands back and lets his wife do all the talking."

A few minutes later, when everyone was indoors, Janey introduced Christina to her husband, Harold, and the two children.

Kimberly was all eyes as she looked up at Christina. "Do you want to see my gifts?" she asked.

"Now don't bother Mrs. Reynolds," Janey told her daughter as she pulled her jacket off of her.

Christina smiled at Kimberly and said, "Yes, I would."

"Goody." She slipped her tiny hand inside of Christina's and led her into the living room.

More cars arrived, and soon Miki found herself surrounded by people who had not made it past the kitchen, as they laughed and chatted and filled their plates with food. She talked with Peter and his wife. They had been in church, although Miki had not seen them in the crowd.

Miki leaned over and whispered to Janey. "Just a small gathering my foot."

Janey grinned. "No one should be alone on this night. No one." She looked seriously into Miki's eyes.

Miki kissed her on the cheek. "I agree, mother hen. I think I'll check on Christina."

"Now who's the mother hen?" Janey teased.

Nearing the living room, Miki could hear an occasional *ooh* and *ahh* from Christina. Kimberly was excitedly describing each of her gifts. Miki picked up two glasses of cider and went in. Christina was on the floor next to the Christmas tree, her legs tucked under her dress, examining a doll.

"She is quite beautiful." She held the doll at arm's length, seriously studying it.

"She's as pretty as you," Kimberly said matter-of-factly.

Christina reached over and touched Kimberly on the cheek. "Well, thank you, Kimberly."

"She is pretty, isn't she, Miki?" Kimberly said of Christina.

Miki felt the heat rising in her cheeks, and she was uncertain what to say.

"Mom says Miki's shy," Kimberly said to Christina as if sharing a grown-up confidence.

"Well, I think your mom's right," Christina smiled up at Miki.

"How about we talk about your gifts?" Miki recovered and handed Christina a glass of cider.

"Thank you."

Miki sat on the floor next to Christina and Kimberly. "Okay?"

"This is my new book." Kimberly picked up the *Beauty and the Beast* and crawled onto Miki's lap. "Will you read it to me?" The top of Kimberly's blond head came just below Miki's chin.

"How about you read it to me?"

"Well, I could," Kimberly said as she leaned her head back

against Miki's shoulder and looked up into her eyes. "But it's more fun if you do it."

"I agree," Christina said a teasing glint in her eyes.

"Don't encourage this scamp." Miki smiled at Christina. "Okay. I tell you what, I'll read two pages and then—"

"Are you bothering Miki?" Harold said as he stepped into the living room.

"She's fine, Harold. We're just negotiating a reading session here." Several other people had entered the room and were admiring the tree and complimenting Harold. Christina stood up and smoothed her dress.

"I tell you what," Miki said softly to Kimberly, "I'll come back and read to you, when we can do it quietly."

"Okay." The youngster bounced off Miki's lap.

"Kimberly, quit bothering Miki," Janey said from the doorway. "Look! Aunt Grace and Uncle Bill brought you and Mark some gifts. By the way, where is Mark?" she glanced around.

"Here, Mom," Mark said from the kitchen, his hands full of cookies.

"You can't eat all those."

"Aw, Mom."

"I'll eat some." Kimberly skipped over to her brother.

Christina reached down and offered Miki her hand. "Here let me help you up."

Miki reached up and felt overwhelmed by the warmth as their hands touched. Christina stood looking up at her.

"Well, Mrs. Reynolds," Peter said appearing out of nowhere. "I didn't know you were here."

Christina turned to smile at the sheriff. "Well, those complaints seem to have led me to a new friend." She smiled at Janey.

"Well, I'm glad, mighty glad," Peter said. "Let me introduce you around."

"Butter wouldn't melt in his mouth," Janey whispered to Miki as she watched Peter, his hand on Christina's elbow, guide her around the room.

"You bet," Miki said softly.

Miki frowned when she heard Scott's voice in the kitchen. Janey murmured. "I invited him, but I didn't think he would come. He was bragging about all the things he was going to do tonight."

"It's fine."

Scott was dressed in a black suit. His pink shirt was out-of-the-package new, his red tie perfectly straight. He looked over the heads of the people he had been talking to and saw Miki. She noted the slight frown before his face turned neutral again.

He came over and shook Miki's hand, then handed a bottle of wine to Janey. "Nice to see you, Ranger."

"Scott."

"Have you eaten?" Janey asked him.

"Yes." Scott laughed. "But I promise to sample something of everything before I leave." He glanced around the room.

"You invited Christina?" Christina still was talking with Peter and his wife. "I'll just go over and say hi."

"Whew, that was fast." Janey turned to welcome the new group of people who had entered her kitchen.

Miki watched Christina say hello to Scott and then peek over at Miki, a tingle of a smile on her lips. Miki was undecided if she should go over when two arms reached up and grabbed her.

"You old son of a gun," Clara Winston said as she hugged her.

"Clara." Miki hugged her former classmate. "This is like reunion week."

Clara pulled Miki back into the kitchen. "You've got to see my kids, all grown up."

For the rest of the evening Miki was distracted by former classmates she hadn't seen in years who wanted to reminisce. Occasionally, she spotted Christina. Scott had not left her side and seemed to be doing most of the talking.

Miki glanced down at her watch.

"I agree, it's late." Christina was quietly by her side, her hand on Miki's arm.

"Would you like to leave?"

"Is it okay?"

"Do you need a ride?" Scott, who had been watching them, walked over and stood between them.

"Yes, as a matter of fact I do." Miki held her breath, wondering whom Christina would choose. "My car is still at the church."

"Well, if you'd like to stay and visit with your old friends, Miki, I'll give Christina a ride."

Christina didn't give Miki a chance to answer. "Well, actually, if Miki doesn't mind, there are some things I'd like to talk over with her." Christina's eyes were imploring.

"I brought the lady," Miki said to Scott. "It's only appropriate I take her back to her car." Miki's intense stare invited no discussion.

"Sure. Maybe we could have lunch someday," he said to Christina. "I could show you Bayport. That's where I live."

"Thanks," Christina said as she turned toward the kitchen. "I'll call you." Christina nodded when she spotted Janey near the stove. "I just want to say good-bye to Janey."

"I'll join you." Miki turned her back on Scott and followed Christina into the kitchen. She reached down and picked up Kimberly, who was still carrying her book.

"Are you going to read to me?"

"I have to take Mrs. Reynolds back to her car, but I promise the next time I'm here I will read the whole book to you."

Kimberly hugged Miki and kissed her cheek. "I like Mrs. Reynolds," she whispered.

Miki looked over to where Christina was hugging Janey. "I'll tell you a secret," Miki said, gazing into fresh green eyes, "I do too."

After saying their good nights, Christina was quiet as she and Miki rode back into town.

"I'm glad I came out. I've been too much of a recluse lately."

"Well, I'm glad you did too." Miki turned right onto Church Street. "What did you want to talk about?"

"Nothing. I just didn't want you to abandon me to Scott. I don't think I could have taken any more cop stories. Do all cops do that?"

"Do what?"

"Talk about themselves and their cases. I notice they never talk about the cases that don't go right."

Miki laughed. "No, they don't. I guess cops are like everybody else. Some brag, some don't." Miki pulled in behind Christina's Mercedes. It was the only car left in front of the church.

"You don't."

Miki felt distracted. "I guess I don't."

"Thank you. I had a wonderful time," Christina said.

"Me too." Miki didn't know how to fill the silence.

"I don't expect you're going to do any kind of surveillance tonight. I doubt that the bad guys would be out on Christmas Eve."

"I doubt it too, but I'm going to follow you home."

"You don't have to do that."

"Ah, but I do," Miki said gently. "I just want to make sure you get home all right, and I'll check to make sure everything is secure."

"Thank you. Actually, I would feel better if you did that. Well, then, see you at the house," Christina said as Miki helped her out of the truck.

Miki followed Christina's Mercedes up her driveway and parked in front as Christina pulled into the three-bay garage. She walked her to the front door.

"Well, Ranger, could I make you a cup of coffee?"

"Thanks, but not tonight."

"Well, then, good night and Merry Christmas," Christina said softly before she turned to let herself in the door.

"Good night."

Miki waited until she heard the click of the lock and then went back to her truck and got her flashlight. She checked each of the first-floor windows and the back door to make sure they were locked. Inside the shed she flashed her light around, then headed for home.

Chapter Six

On Christmas Day Miki busied herself with chores around the cabin. She didn't talk to Christina all day. She went to bed early and set her alarm for eleven p.m. She got up and made her way to Christina's house around midnight.

She buried her snowmobile in the woods and skirted along the edge of the property so she could stay in the shadow of the trees. The surveillance was much easier now that she was using Christina's shed.

Tonight, she was feeling frustration and impatience that the case remained unsolved. She walked the short distance to the shed. The minute she entered she sensed she was not alone. Miki reached for her gun.

"I'm sorry, I expected to be out of here by the time you arrived." Christina's voice sounded nervous in the dark night.

Miki reached in her jacket for her penlight, cupped her hand around the bulb and turned it on. Christina was standing near the table, a plate still in her hand.

Christina laughed self-consciously. "I feel like I've been caught with my hand in the cookie jar, but I wanted the food to be hot."

"Mrs. Reynolds, this is no time for a picnic."

"You're angry." Christina stared down at her hands.

"No, not angry. Frustrated. Frustrated that nothing has happened with this case."

"Well, I thought at least you could be comfortably fed. It may be late, but it's still Christmas." Christina motioned toward the table. "Food is part of my social—" Christina stopped. "But of course I'm being silly. You're not here to be social. I'm sorry."

Miki unzipped her snowmobile suit. It was warm in the heated shed. "It's okay. I'm sorry. I'm taking my frustration out on you tonight." Miki looked down at all the dishes and shook her head. "It looks like there's enough food here to feed me and half the bad guys in town. Look, why don't we move this inside where we can talk. I'll just bag the surveillance tonight."

She picked up some of the dishes and helped Christina carry them into the kitchen. Once inside, she stood awkwardly at the door, uncertain what to do. Christina put her serving dishes on the table and reached for Miki's.

"Come on, sit down, get out of that warm suit. You're going to roast in it."

Miki unzipped the one-piece suit and slipped out of it. She adjusted her collar and tucked her shirt into her uniform pants. Christina busied herself with putting place mats, plates and dinnerware on the table.

"What would you like to drink? I have stuff that is stronger than coffee."

"Coffee is fine."

Christina gestured to the table. "Sit." She lifted up the tops to the serving dishes. "Lobster stew, peas, hot rolls . . ." Christina shrugged. "Somehow today when I was preparing it I didn't feel quite as foolish as I do now. You must think me—"

Miki laughed. "It's fine. Let's just say you've introduced a whole new concept to surveillance. It isn't usually like going to a five-star restaurant."

"Thank you." Christina's black eyes stared into Miki's. "You believed me, and for that I will always be grateful. For a time I felt like I was losing it." Christina seemed suddenly far away. Miki was silent. Miki wondered at how close Christina had come to running back to Boston. "Speaking of believing, Scott stopped in today. Said he didn't want me to be alone on Christmas Day."

Miki stopped eating, a spoonful of lobster stew just inches from her mouth. "What did he want?"

Christina looked at a spot over Miki's head. "I really don't know. He got here around three this afternoon. As a matter of fact I was in the kitchen making the lobster stew. Came in, sat right where you're sitting and said he wanted to . . . chat. So we chatted."

"What exactly did he want to chat about?"

"Well"—Christina wiped a drop of stew from her lip— "mostly he chatted and I listened. About himself. Someday plans to be sheriff, stuff about renovating his house. Things like that."

"Did he ask you anything about the investigation?"

"Some. Wanted to know if you stayed long last night. I told him no."

Miki frowned.

Christina stopped eating. "Did I do something wrong?"

"No. But in the future, I'd prefer that you not mention that I'm here at night. Telling Scott is fine, he's a law enforcement officer, but I'd rather you not mention it to anyone else."

Christina held up her right hand as if swearing an oath. "I haven't told another living sole. Not even my husband—well, actually ex-husband. He called today to wish me a Merry Christmas and scold me for not returning to Boston."

"Well, you can tell him if you'd like."

"I'd rather not. He'd want to do that male protective thing, and he'd be here in a second. I don't want that right now." Christina studied her nails.

"Christina, if you'd like I could bring Scott up to speed on what I'm doing, and he could take over the surveillance and the investigation." Miki could feel a drop in her mood. She leaned her chin against the back of her hand as she waited for Christina to respond.

"No," Christina said a little too sharply. "Look," she said her tone softening, "I admit I did feel uncomfortable around you at first, but not"—Christina held up her hand— "because you're a woman, but because you're rather formal. I felt like this useless female being protected by, of all things, another female."

"I'm sorry."

"Don't say it. I'm glad. I like you, Ranger Mik. I thank you for believing me, and I definitely want you on this case."

Miki hesitated, uncertain what to say.

Christina broke the silence. "More stew?"

"Please."

The rest of the night they talked about books, music and Boston. Miki got the distinct impression that Christina was surprised when she spoke about Bach instead of the Beasties, and when they discussed Carol Shields' Pulitzer Prize–winning novel, *The Stone Diaries.* and not *Field and Stream.*

Miki looked at her watch. "Wow. It's four a.m. Let me help you with the dishes."

Christina pointed at the wall. "Dishwasher."

Miki put on her snowmobile suit. "I've enjoyed myself." She turned and looked at Christina. "Thank you."

"So have I," Christina said. "I'd like to do this again."

"Me too, but not during my surveillance time. My boss would frown on it if he knew I was sitting inside instead of being outside catching the perps."

"Perps?"

"Perpetrators."

"Right."

Miki stood awkwardly near the door.

A smile tugged at Christina's lips. "I guess I'll have to make the first overture." She held out her hand and shook Miki's. "Thank you for having dinner with me. I would like to do it again."

Christina's eyes looked like lush sable. "That's a hint, Ranger. Now you're supposed to invite me to dinner."

Miki felt the blush creeping up her neck again. "Would you like to have dinner with me?"

"Yes, I would." Christina's touch was warm, intoxicating. Miki did not like what she was feeling.

"When?"

"Um . . ." Miki did an instant flash forward on her mental calendar. She had to be back in Jackman for two days at the end of the week for a trial. "How about Saturday night? I have to be in Jackman on Thursday and Friday."

"You're leaving." Christina dropped Miki's hand. Concern etched across her face. She pushed her hands down into the front of her wool white slacks.

"Just for two days. I have a deer-jacking case that goes to trial Thursday, the assistant district attorney up there has assured me it won't go more than two days, maybe one if the guy cops a plea."

"More lingo. Deer-jacking?

"Deer-jacking is when a hunter shines a spotlight on a deer at night. The deer freezes in its tracks, and the hunter shoots it like a fish in a bowl."

"How ghastly."

"And illegal. How about Saturday?"

"Saturday? That's New Year's Eve."

"Fabulous. There's a nice restaurant in town. I'll make reservations."

Christina hesitated. "I know this might seem quite foolish, but if something should happen and I would have to get in touch with you, is there—" Christina stopped, clearly embarrassed.

"Call dispatch. They can reach me day or night anywhere. And Christina, don't hesitate to do it. I'm only two hours away, and I can be here PDQ." She smiled. "Pretty damn quick."

Christina tried to hide her concern. "I'm being silly. New Year's Eve. Yes, I'd like to have dinner with you then."

"Good. I'll make reservations and pick you up on the snowmobile at seven p.m."

"Snowmobile?"

"There is this terrific restaurant, but it is in the boonies. You can go by car, but most of us zip over on our snowmobiles. Would you prefer the truck?"

"Snowmobile?" Christina said the word as if for the first time. "Snowmobile it is. I've never been on one."

"Good, then it'll be a new adventure. One that requires you to dress warmly."

"You're on, Ranger." Christina touched Miki's arm. "And thank you."

Miki felt a lump in her throat. "You're welcome." She opened the door, and a blast of cold air hit her face. She wanted to reach down into the snowbank, scoop up a handful and press it against her face. She needed to cool off.

Chapter Seven

Miki got up early Wednesday morning. She felt restless. The cabin seemed smaller than usual. She put on her down vest and went outside. In the past, splitting wood had been therapeutic, and she'd probably split a full cord before she could relax.

She tossed the pieces onto a pile. Ordinarily the rhythmic act of splitting and tossing would assuage her frustrations, but not today. Thoughts of Christina dominated every moment. She had spent a sleepless night, but she knew she needed to stay focused. There had been two more surveillances and still no results. She hadn't seen Christina since Christmas Day, but evidence of her presence was in the shed each night she had returned. She welcomed the separation if only for two days. She was leaving for Jackman tonight.

The sun felt wonderful on her skin. She lifted each of the rounds onto the splitting block and with the precision of a surgeon raised the splitting maul high over her head and let the weight swing smartly to bury the cutting edge into the center of the wood.

With her left hand, she lifted a mallet over her head and hit the flat edge of the maul, driving it through the center of the log like a knife through bread. She fell into a rhythm—lift the round, a single quick blow into the center with the maul and a sharp rap with the mallet.

Despite the cold, the sweat trickled down her chest and back. Her face was smudged from where she brushed dirty hands against her cheeks. She had long since abandoned her vest. She turned at the sound of the car. The black Mercedes parked just behind her truck.

Elegant in her lavender jacket and matching lavender slacks, Christina stepped out of the car. Not for the first time, Miki felt like a giant next to her. She laid the maul down.

"Don't let me interrupt. I was just wondering if you'd like to have dinner tonight."

"I can't. I'm leaving for Jackman tonight. I have to be in court early tomorrow morning. But we still are on for dinner Saturday night, right?."

Christina frowned. "Of course . . . Of course we still are on for dinner Saturday night." But she looked disappointed. She looked around. "You split your own wood?"

Miki reached down and threw the evenly sliced quarters onto her woodpile. "Yup."

"Splitting wood. I never really thought about it, but I guess someone has to do it. I always figured wood was like pork chops, something already sliced up and packaged."

Miki laughed. "Well, in some cases that's true. But most people around here split their own. Some with a mechanical wood splitter, but most with a splitting maul." Miki held it up so Christina could examine it.

"Does it hurt?"

"Well, the first few days, your muscles are pretty sore, but after that, it actually feels pretty good."

"Could I try?"

"Well."

"You think I'm too wimpy?"

"Well, you're a little overdressed and it's pretty heavy."

Christina slipped off her jacket, revealing a white silk blouse. "Well, I'd still like to try." She held out her hand. Miki passed her the splitting maul, which Christina held like a golf club.

"Here, let me show you." Miki demonstrated. "You hold it more like a baseball bat." Christina reached for the maul and repositioned her hands the way Miki had showed her. Miki picked a soft wood log from the pile and stood it on end on the splitting block. "What you want to do is bring the maul down smack in the middle of the log. It will split in two."

Christina lifted the maul over her head, the weight pulling down on her arms, grit her teeth and swung. The maul glanced off the top of the log and knocked it to the ground unsplit. Miki didn't say a word.

"I expect it takes some practice."

Miki picked up a large round maple stump and set it on the splitting block. She raised the maul over her head, her shoulders tense, the muscles of her arms putting weight behind the swing, and dropped the maul right in the middle, splitting it in half.

Christina shook her head. "You make it look easy."

"Well, I've been doing it since I was a kid."

"Could I try again?"

Miki again placed the soft birch onto the splitting block. "Now, hold your hands as though you were swinging a baseball bat over your head." Miki demonstrated. "And let the weight of the maul do the work."

Christina, her jaw tight, grasped the wooden handle and raised the maul over her head and let it fly. It hit right in the center, slicing the birch log in half.

"Yahoo," Christina hooted.

Miki laughed. "Very good."

Christina leaned against the maul. "Now, why don't you put a real piece of wood up there. I may be city, but I ain't stupid." She teased.

"Yes, ma'am. Feeling scrappy?" Miki placed a piece of rock maple on the splitting block.

Christina lifted the maul high over her head and let it slam down into the round. But this time the maul bounced off the top, and the wood fell onto the ground uncut.

"Ouch." Christina rubbed her shoulders.

Miki knew the feeling—the vibrations travel straight up the arms. "Even with frost in them, hardwood logs are buggers to split."

Christina leaned over, picked up the maple log and placed it back on the splitting block. "I can do it," she said quietly. She brushed a bead of sweat from her forehead, leaving a smudge. Her muscles tightened with determination and the tip of the maul bit evenly into the center. "Wow."

Miki laughed. "Very good." She handed Christina the mallet. "Now take this, hold the handle of the maul and hit the broad side of the maul with this, and it will split the wood the rest of the way."

Christina felt the weight of the mallet. She looked doubtful. "One arm?"

"If you don't hold on to the maul's handle, it will jump off the block when you hit it, and it could hit you."

Feet apart, looking every bit as determined as she was with the splitting maul, Christina lifted the mallet over her head. Miki held her breath. Christina let the mallet swing evenly down and dead center onto the maul. The maple block split in half.

"Far out." Christina was ebullient. She grabbed Miki by the arm and held it. Her eyes were sexy, inviting. She was breathing hard from the exertion.

Miki was silent. She had been watching Christina and she wanted to hug her, to feel her skin against hers. Miki shook off the image and said finally, "That was great. You're going to be mighty sore tomorrow though."

"Can I help some more?"

"Sure, but tell you what, I'll split and you toss."

"Toss?"

"Pick up each split end and throw it on that pile over there."

"Agreed."

They worked together in silence. Miki couldn't shake off the image of Christina, her arms high over her head, her breasts straining against the front of her silk blouse, half moons of sweat staining under her arms. She put more force and energy into each swing and felt the vibration in her shoulders as the maul connected with the wood. She stopped to catch her breath, and Christina stopped too.

"You're pretty fierce there, determined."

Miki smiled. "Good therapy."

"Therapy?"

"People spend thousands of dollars talking to someone about their pent-up frustrations. All they need to do is split a few cords of wood, and I guarantee you frustration will fly out the window."

"Are you frustrated?"

Miki sighed. "Sometimes."

"What frustrates you?"

Miki stared at Christina. There were more smudges on her face. Pieces of bark that had flown off the wood hung from her hair. She wanted to reach over and rub a finger against the smudges. Miki swallowed. "Your situation for one thing. I feel as though I'm getting nowhere."

"Well, the night problems have stopped."

"But I'm not sure if this is permanent or if someone has figured out that I'm watching. I was thinking, when I get back from Jackman I may try something different."

"What do you want to do?"

"Let me just chew on it a few days. If it works in my head I'll tell you about it. Okay?"

"Okay." Christina reached out her hand. "Can I try that splitting part. I'd like to dump some of my frustrations."

"Sure, here." Miki handed her the maul. Christina turned her back to Miki and set a maple stump on the splitting block. Miki watched her fluid movements and swallowed. She turned away and looked out across her property, but she could not escape the woman's quiet allure. She was resolved. She was determined to solve this case and get back to Jackman.

Chapter Eight

Although she was packed to leave, Miki wanted to check Christina's property one more time. She threw a thermos of coffee in her backpack and pulled the snowmobile out of the lean-to. She went east toward the lake and decided to run a parallel track with it. That way she could check to see if there were any fresh tracks between the lake and the house. It was a trip she had made before. But this time, instead of focusing on the scenery and the rhythmic blip of the trees as she sped past them, she thought about Christina and the day they had spent together. There had been something flirtatiously exciting and dangerously inviting. They had kept up a rhythmic pace, splitting and tossing, and in between, talking. Christina talked about life in Boston.

After she and Christina finished splitting wood, they sat in Miki's cabin, drinking coffee and talking. Christina told her about her ex-husband, John, an advertising account executive who had worked for her father. They had been married for ten years. There were no children. For her, the decision to not have children was easy; she didn't want to have any until some kind of normalcy entered her life. John was too busy proving he could make it in the advertising world, even though he had married the boss's daughter, a daughter who also was an ambitious account executive in her father's firm. They kept saying they would wait. Then, Christina's father died unexpectedly and she left Boston because there was pressure on her to take over the family business. Then she was her husband's boss. And, for the first time, Christina told Miki, she faced what had been lurking underneath their picture-perfect marriage. The marriage splintered. The spirit and energy that had drawn them together had been channeled into their careers, rather than to a life together. Miki had let Christina talk.

Miki shut off the snowmobile and walked toward the beach. She knew the good weather would have drawn fishermen there. She looked at her watch. One hour to sundown. If they were there, they'd be gathering up their gear, ready to head home.

Miki saw the trucks, then noticed the police cruiser with its engine running. She knew it was Scott even before she looked across the lake. Although she hadn't seen him since Christmas Eve, he was like a pop-up video in her imagination, there and then gone. It had taken her days to identify her feelings. She resented how he had dominated Christina's time at Janey's party. Jealousy was creeping all over her. Miki thought about the silly rhyme she and her high school friends used to chant. She recalled those few anxious moments the night he had offered to take Christina home. She had held her breath like a kid. She had wanted Christina to choose her over him, and when she did she felt like she had won something. Yikes, she thought, she was jealous of a straight man who was interested in a straight woman. It must be all this lake air, Miki bit at her thoughts. I am not interested in Christina. She repeated the phrase like a mantra.

A large stand of trees obscured her view of the lake, but she could hear male voices. The land jutted out toward the ice shacks, and she walked closer to where Scott and the men were talking. A few feet to her right, there was a small rise and a tiny break in the trees. She could see Scott; he was zipping up his heavy brown jacket and pulling his collar up around his ears. Three of the men were seated around a makeshift campfire built on a metal base; a pot of coffee hung from a tripod at its center. Miki knew Jacob Smith, who worked at the paper mill in Downey. His brother-in-law, Clarence Sparks, was across from him, a mug of coffee balanced on his knee.

She remembered the third man, Billy Clark. Miki watched as he sharpened his knife on a whetstone. Keith Shipman was leaning against one of the ice shacks. He owned the garage and service station where the county had its cars serviced.

"Haven't seen you fellas around much," Miki heard Scott say.

"Been here most days," Jacob said. "Back on night shift."

Clarence Sparks spit tobacco between his teeth. It landed on the fire. He usually let his brother-in-law do the talking.

"Haven't seen you around much either, Scott," Keith tossed out. He looked over at Jacob, and the two men exchanged a look. "You been replaced by a woman?" Keith's teasing tone had a sharp bite to it.

Miki winced. Regardless of her feelings toward Scott, being replaced on a case was bad, being replaced by a woman must be a real ego stomper. Maybe, she thought, she should bring him in on the case. She gave a mental shrug. This is too much. First I hate him because I'm jealous; now I feel sorry for him.

"I figure she won't be here long." Miki watched Scott shove his hands in his pockets.

"How so?" Jacob asked.

"Simple. If whoever is doing this really scares the woman, she'll want a real cop around, not some tree hugger ranger from up north."

"Why you off the case?"

"Mrs. Reynolds called the governor. No one tells the governor what to do. But me and the sheriff, we see this as just some harmless fun. Anyone serious about doing something would do something big to scare her. These have been just pranks. Probably kids."

"Ain't right what that city lady's doing," Clarence Sparks spoke for the first time. "Trying to keep us off our fishing lake. We been here longer than her. She comes in here, puts up signs, and orders us around. Maybe if one of those kids scare her enough she'll go back to Boston and leave us alone."

"Well now"—Scott chose his words carefully— "what I figure we have is an access problem. Hell, I figure I could talk her into letting everything go back like it was. You wanna fish, you can cross her land. You know these city women; you gotta be kinda gentle with them."

Hell, no use hiding in the trees, Miki thought as she watched the men. Might as well give them all a good scare.

"You think she would give in?" Jacob asked.

"You know women. Think one thing today, and their head is somewhere else tomorrow," Scott chuckled.

Keith, who had been divorced for five years, said. "Go figure."

"Billy was telling us—" Jacob stopped when he saw Miki. "Hey, Ranger."

Scott turned in surprise.

"Scott." Miki nodded to the other men. "How's the wife and kids, Jacob?"

"Just fine, Ranger," Jacob was visibly unsettled by Miki's sudden appearance.

"Been here long?" Scott recovered quickly. Miki knew he was wondering how much she had heard.

"Just got here. Was checking some of the trails." She looked to where the sun was just a tiny orange slice in the sky. "Going to be dark soon."

Jacob looked at his watch. "Gotta get going." He picked up the coffeepot and dumped it on the fire. The rest watched the fire first hiss and than smoke.

"Glad you're here, Ranger," Keith said, picking up some of his gear. "Billy here was telling us all something real interesting. Says some of that land's his. Said if he got it, he'd let us cross it."

"That so?" Miki asked, looking at Billy.

Billy nodded.

"His daddy was caretaker for that city lady's granddaddy." Jacob stopped pushing fishing items in a bag long enough to contribute. "Says old Mr. Reynolds promised his granddaddy the land."

"That true, Billy?" Miki persisted.

Billy didn't look up. "That's what my daddy told me."

"How much land?" Scott asked.

Billy shrugged. "Ten acres."

"You got anything in writing?" Miki asked.

"Nope."

"Well, I figure," Keith joined in, "it gives a man powerful reason to want to get it. I told Billy he should haul her into court for stealing his land."

"Well, that's okay, but you need proof." Miki said. "Your daddy still alive?"

Billy shook his head no.

"That's a tough one. No deed." Scott joined in. "Unless you got something in writing, no one's going to listen."

"I think he should just take it." Keith persisted. "Not in a bad way. Just go squat on the land. That'd create a ruckus. Maybe upset the woman enough, she'd go home."

Miki didn't like the way the conversation was going. "Look. You can't just take land. I'll talk with Mrs. Reynolds, tell her what you believe to be true." she looked directly at Billy. Miki didn't like the way Keith seemed to be steering the conversation. There was a meanspiritedness to what she hoped was teasing. She could not read Billy. His one-syllable answers did not give her any indication what he was thinking.

"You won't be able to do that until you get back?" Scott interjected. Miki frowned; she had told no one except Christina she was leaving. "Heard you have to be in Jackman tonight. Don't you have a case going up there in court tomorrow?"

"Yeah, I do." She glared at Scott.

"Janey told me." Scott offered. "Said if I see you to tell you that the court clerk called, said it looked like the case would take at least

61

two days. Maybe even kick over until Monday if the jury can't reach a decision."

"Regardless, when I get back," Miki addressed her remarks to Billy. "I'll talk with Mrs. Reynolds. I promise."

"Won't do no good." Keith offered. "He ain't got no paper. Like I said, I think he ought to take it."

"Keith, I'm going to say this only once." Miki began quietly. "No one is going to take anything. Now when I get back, I will talk with Mrs. Reynolds."

"That's right, boys." Scott joined in. "It's against the law to take land that doesn't belong to you. Let the ranger here handle it when she gets back. But . . ." he paused. "I gotta agree with Keith. If you don't have anything in writing, Billy, I doubt she'll listen."

Miki glared at Scott. The few seconds that she had felt sorry for him were gone. Now she just wanted to close his mouth.

"Well, I got to get back to the office." Scott turned away from Miki. "See you men around. I'll see you when you get back, Miki." He called over his shoulder.

Jacob and Keith were storing their gear in the ice shack.

Billy closed the knife he had been sharpening and stuck it in his pocket. He nodded to Miki. She watched him climb into an old Chevy.

"You think it's right?" Jacob asked Miki, picking up the thread of conversation. He also watched Billy get into his car.

"I think we need to remain calm and let me talk with Mrs. Reynolds," Miki said.

"Well, I hope you can do something," Keith joined in. "But I got a bad feeling. People ain't happy, and when they ain't happy, things happen."

Miki stared hard at the fisherman. "You suggesting something might happen?"

Keith turned away from Miki's stare. "I'm just saying things aren't right. And somebody better fix them. See ya, Ranger." Keith carried his gear to his car.

"Jacob, I've known you a long time. You hearing anything?"

"Naw. That's just Keith. You know how he likes to blow hot. Hour from now, he'll be at home watching TV, not even remembering what he was blustering about. Don't worry, Miki; he's just talk."

"I hope so," she walked with Jacob and Clarence to their car. "You hear anything, you call me, hear?"

"You got it." Miki watched as they drove off. She felt the first stir of evening air. It was going to be another cold night. Miki shivered. Somehow, she knew it wasn't from the cold.

Chapter Nine

The trial lasted two days, and although Miki wanted to bolt as soon as the case went to the jury, she had to stay until the end. She glanced at her watch. Eight p.m. and the jury still was out. Everyone seemed anxious to get home for New Year's weekend.

She thought about Christina and wondered what she was doing. The woman had entered her thoughts at least a thousand times since she left. More if she counted the drive up. Several times she picked up the phone to call her, but she had forced herself not to. She had called dispatch; no reports of problems. She'd also called Janey, who said she had not heard from Christina.

Miki slumped deeper in her chair. It wasn't an attraction, she told herself. It couldn't be. Not for a straight woman. Something was radically wrong. Christina was in the danger zone, and Miki did not want to go there.

Straight, straight, straight, she silently repeated to herself. This was her second mantra in just two days. Straight, straight, straight.

"Hey," Jeff Stinger said. "Just got word from the judge. The jury is on its way in." Miki was startled, as if she had been yanked away from a hypnotic dream. She noticed that the defendant and his attorney were back at the defense table.

Miki rose to her feet as the bailiff knocked on the door. "All rise. The Honorable Judge Caroline Heart presiding."

"Both counsels ready?"

The attorneys' twin answers: "Yes, Your Honor."

The judge nodded to the bailiff. "You may bring them in." Miki watched as the eight women and four men filed quietly into the jury box.

"Be seated," she told the courtroom. "Madam foreman, have you reached a verdict?"

"Yes, Your Honor." She handed a piece of paper to the bailiff, who carried it to the judge.

Judge Heart studied the paper, then nodded to the court clerk. "You may inquire."

"On the single charge of illuminating wildlife, how do you say?" the clerk asked.

"Guilty." Miki stopped listening as each of the remaining charges was read and the foreman responded "guilty."

The judge thanked the jurors and told them they could leave.

Jeff patted her on the back. "Good case," he whispered to Miki.

After the courtroom had been cleared of jurors, the judge requested a presentence report from the Department of Probation and Parole, which the defense attorney and prosecutor agreed to. At last they were recessed.

"Have time for dinner?" Jeff said to Miki as he stuffed papers into his briefcase.

"Naw, I really have to get back."

"Ah, come on. My wife is out of town, and besides, you can be back there in two hours, less if you hop to it. Please?"

Miki grinned. "All right. But let's go somewhere where we can get a quick meal."

Later, Miki sighed as she looked at the clock in her truck. She and Jeff had talked for hours about cases they had handled together. When she finally got on the road it was midnight. She had hoped to be back at the cabin earlier.

As the miles clipped by, Miki was lulled by the rhythm of the road. It hadn't snowed for two days, so the pavement was plowed and for the most part dry. Miki felt her pager vibrate against her hip. She pulled it off her belt and looked at the number.

She hurriedly reached for her cell phone and dialed the Jefferson County dispatcher. The cellular phone clicked and then gave a busy signal. Miki looked at the illuminated dial on the top of the phone and saw a symbol that indicated she was out of range. The next town was ten minutes away. Miki reached up and flipped on her blue lights. Within minutes she was standing beside a closed Rite Aid drug store, the pay phone cold in her hand. She pulled her collar up around her ears as she listened to the telephone ring.

The dispatcher answered. "Miki. Glad we got you. There's been a problem at the Reynolds place. You said to call—"

"What kind of trouble?"

"Someone tried to break in. Miki, they had a gun."

Miki swore under her breath. "Who's there?"

"The sheriff, Scott. Several deputies have been out searching."

Miki gripped the top of the telephone with her free hand. "Anyone hurt?"

"Negative. She's pretty shaken up, not crying, mostly mad. The sheriff tried to get her to go the hospital, but she refused. She's been yelling for you. Called for you three times, twice after Scott and the sheriff arrived."

"This is the first page." Miki frowned.

"Paged you two times before, but you apparently were out of range. I even called the courthouse and the D.A.'s office up there, but I kept missing you."

Miki looked at her watch. "I can be there in a half-hour to forty-five minutes. Call Mrs. Reynolds and tell her I'm on my way."

"Okay. And Mik, be careful. As you get closer to the coast the temperature is dropping. We've had cars off the road because of black ice."

"Thanks, Joey."

Miki hooked her seat belt and would have peeled rubber out of the driveway had it not been covered with snow. She turned off her radio. It was time to concentrate on the road.

Miki could see the flashing lights through the trees at the entrance to Christina's driveway. The blue strobes had a rhythmic pulse like the *blip blip blip* of a heart monitor.

She eased her truck in behind the sheriff's vehicle. Deputies, their large flashlights bobbing up and down, were searching the woods around the house. Probably obliterating any useful footprints, Miki groused.

The door opened as she stepped up onto the porch, and Christina fell into her arms. Her flushed face felt hot against Miki's neck. "I'm so glad you're here."

Miki held the woman in her arms. She felt her relax, then she felt the tears against her neck.

"God, I promised myself I wouldn't cry."

She looked over Christina's head and saw Scott. The two officers glared at each other. Miki saw a sudden look of understanding creep over his eyes and just as quickly leave, replaced by an icy stare.

The wind was at her back. She put one arm around Christina and gently guided her inside. She kicked the door closed with her foot.

Peter, who had been in the kitchen, came into the room and said, "Glad you're here. Mrs. Reynolds has had a heck of a scare tonight."

"What happened?" Christina would not let go of her.

He nodded to a window near the piano, where the curtains were blowing from the open window. "Mrs. Reynolds said she heard a noise and came down. She caught the subject with his head already through the window. He had a gun. She couldn't tell what kind. Says she screamed and scared the guy. My guys are out there searching for him now. I told her I'd keep deputies here for the rest of the night. Scott's offered to stay right here in the house with her. There's no question someone tried to break in."

"Christina," Miki said as she eased her onto the sofa. "Are you all right?"

She nodded yes and wiped her tears with her sleeve.

"Peter, how about a glass of water."

"Offered it to her. Won't take it."

"Miki, I just want this nightmare to go away."

"It will, Christina, I promise." Miki turned to the sheriff. "Your deputies find anything outside?"

"Footprints to and from the house. Scott said they seemed to just disappear into the night."

Miki frowned. "Seems strange."

As if on cue, Scott cleared his throat. "Not really, haven't had any new snow around here for days. The stuff that's there is iced over, and it's hard to find footprints."

"A man moving fast would leave deep impressions in the snow," Miki mused.

"Yeah, well, it's pretty tromped over out there, what with the deputies and all," he persisted.

"I asked Mrs. Reynolds if she could come into the office tomorrow and give us a statement. I'll take it myself. I think she needs to calm down now," Peter said to Miki.

"I agree. Look, why don't you post men at the front and back."

"You're not going to leave are you?" Christina gripped her hand.

"I promise." Miki said when she saw the fear in Christina's eyes. "I'll stay right here in the house." Christina slumped back against the sofa. For the first time that night she seemed to relax.

"Christina," Miki said softly. "I'm going to talk to the sheriff and Scott outside. Then—"

Christina had a vise grip on her arm. "Please come back."

"In just a minute." Miki rubbed the tops of Christina's hands, then followed the sheriff and Scott out of the door.

"Looks like you got—" Miki's leveled a stare at Scott that made him clip his words mid-sentence.

Peter didn't seem to notice. He glared back at the house.

"How'd he get the window open?" Miki addressed her question to the sheriff, ignoring Scott.

"Broke the pane just below the lock. Reached in and opened it. That's what Mrs. Reynolds heard when she thought something had been thrown against the house. Of course, that's what she's heard before. Look, I think it's a good idea you stay here and I'll post men at the front and back."

"Okay . . . Funny"—Miki looked out across Christina's front lawn, now covered over with a thin sheen of ice over thick snow—"that he'd try something tonight. You'd wonder if he was casing the place or something."

"Naw, I don't think he'd be that bright. Just one of the locals trying to give her a scare," Peter said. "Heck of a scare. Guy wore a ski mask. Although I admit I don't like the idea that a gun was used. She said she didn't see the whole thing, only what she thought was a barrel."

"That's a good enough description for me. She says it was a gun, I believe her," Miki frowned at the sheriff challenging him to disagree with her.

"Look, this isn't the time to probably bring this up, but understand you been running surveillance here. I wish you'd told me. I could've put some of my deputies on it while you were gone. We might have caught him."

Miki clenched her jaws. "Maybe." She wasn't going to talk about this in front of Scott. She noted the smirk on his face, and she stuck her hands in her pockets. It wouldn't do to deck a deputy sheriff.

Peter waited for Miki to say more. "Will you bring her over in the morning?"

"I will."

The sheriff called two of his deputies over and spoke to them. Scott stood staring at Miki, and she met his unwavering gaze.

When Peter finished talking to the two deputies he turned back to Miki. "This has moved beyond a practical joke," he said as he pulled his collar tighter around his neck. The temperature had dropped during the time they'd been standing there. "We don't have home invasions here, not in my county. I promise you we'll catch this guy."

"No question, Peter." Miki felt drained, and she was really tired of the sheriff and his deputy. "But right now I think we have to make certain that Mrs. Reynolds is safe."

"Look," Peter said. "You look beat. Why don't you go home, and I'll get one of the female correction officers from the jail to come over and spend the rest of the night here."

"It's okay. Mrs. Reynolds knows me. I think she'd feel less anxious if I stayed."

"Well, you do what you think is right. If you want a female deputy here at other times, just let me know."

"I'll know more after tomorrow." Miki looked up at the clouds, black and angry. There would be more snow tonight. "The colonel is not going to be happy with me. I think he thought I'd have the guy by now. Who knows, he might pull me off the case."

"That'd be a mistake," Peter interjected. "Right now you're the only one she trusts. I wouldn't worry too much about the colonel. I'll call him in the morning, tell him what happened and that we're now working closely with you on this."

"Thanks, Peter." She felt relief envelope her. Peter was upset, but he was a friend and had cut her some slack. A better friend than she had been. "Look, I'd better get back inside."

The sheriff reached up and patted Miki on the shoulder. "Come by tomorrow. We'll talk about how we can catch this scumball."

70

Christina had not moved from the sofa. Miki took off her jacket and laid it in a chair. "Why don't we go into the kitchen and I'll get you a cup of coffee."

"I was so scared," Christina said, her eye blurred by tears. "I've never felt so helpless and scared in my life."

Miki knelt next to her. "Come here," she said softly, opening her arms.

Christina laid her head against Miki's shoulder and sobbed. Angry at herself for leaving her alone, Miki stroked her hair. She should have trusted Peter and gotten him to assign a deputy to take over the surveillance while she was gone. Miki tightened her arms around Christina. She had screwed up, and now someone she was falling for was suffering.

The sobs turned into hiccups. "I'm sorry." Christina pulled her face away from Miki's shoulder. "I've gotten your shirt all wet," she said between hiccups.

As Miki looked at her she felt a rush of desire surge, and she quickly pushed it away. "Christina, I'm so sorry. I never should have left you alone. I should have gotten another deputy to watch the place. This is my fault," she confessed.

"Who'd have thought he'd come when you weren't here?" Christina frowned.

Miki leaned back on her heels. "Scott knew." She focused on what had been nagging at her since she had gotten the message from the dispatcher. "The day I left he was down talking with the ice fishermen. He made it known I'd be gone. I'm not saying one of them did it, but once talk is out there, it knows no boundaries." Miki took Christina's hand. "I've really screwed up and put you in danger. I should have told Peter so he could have assigned deputies to watch your house. Look, if you want me off the case, I understand."

Christina looked deep into Miki's eyes. "You can't leave. I can't remember the last time I needed someone like this." Christina touched Miki's cheek. "I feel"—she paused— "safe with you. You believed me when no one else would. Do you understand how important that is to me? And besides, I thought we were becoming friends." Christina looked at her quizzically.

Miki felt a warm flush rise from her toes. "I'm here, Christina and I promise you I'll catch him." She stood up. She needed some movement to break the tension or she would have pulled Christina into her arms, bathed her in kisses. "How about some coffee?" she offered distractedly.

"I think I'd rather just go to bed. Will you come with me? You won't leave me?"

"No. I'll be right here the rest of the night."

Miki followed Christina up the stairs to her room. She noticed for the first time that Christina had on a yellow silk robe and that it swayed against her slender ankles.

There was a king-size bed in the bedroom; the covers had been hastily pushed aside. Christina slipped out of her robe and slippers and sat on the side of the bed.

"I don't ever recall being this tired," Christina murmured.

Miki held up the covers on the bed and Christina slipped underneath. "Christina, I'll be downstairs. If you hear a noise or need a glass of water, I'll be here in a second. I sleep very lightly."

Christina smiled. "Thank you."

Miki wanted to push Christina's hair back, stroke her high cheekbones and trace a finger across her lips. Instead she reached over and tuned off the lamp next to Christina's bed. "Good night."

As she descended the stairs, Miki felt an inner turmoil. There was a battle between her need to protect and her desire to comfort. She had covered other cases where a woman had cried on her shoulder, but this was the first time she had felt a jolt of desire. She could almost hear Kristan say, "You're being a fool, Miki Jamieson."

Miki put her coat on and went to her truck and got her flashlight. She saw the deputy, his car parked halfway up the driveway, the engine idling to keep him warm. She turned on her flashlight and walked to the window that had been forced open by the intruder and later nailed shut by one of the deputies. A towel was jammed into the space where the windowpane was broken.

The snow on the ground near the window had been trampled, any footprints trod upon by cops too anxious to do their job.

Around to the back, another deputy leaned against a tree. "You're going to freeze out here." Miki said to Jimmy Cates. "You can watch the house from in here," she nodded toward the shed.

"Thanks. It was getting mighty cold."

He followed Miki into the shed. She used her flashlight to locate the space heater and clicked it on. "It'll be warm in a few minutes."

"This is bad, Miki. I feel sorry for her." Miki couldn't see his eyes in the dark, but she could hear the concern in his voice. "I don't even want to think about what he might have had in mind."

"Me neither," Miki said softly. "Me neither."

She continued her walk around the house. She checked the back door; it was locked. She then went back to the front and inside.

After shutting off most of the lights in the living room, she eyed the white sofa but couldn't bring herself to lie down on its pristine upholstery. She slipped off her boots and then pulled off her shirt, rolled it into a ball and laid it on the floor. She took off her gun belt and set it next to her shirt. "Pretend you're camping," she said to herself.

Lying down, she pulled her coat over herself and thought about Christina. Miki needed to turn this event into a positive, and she knew just the person who could help her do it. She shifted uncomfortably on the floor. "Pretend you're camping," she told her body. Minutes later she was asleep.

The next morning, Miki stood next to Christina in the kitchen, watching her make the coffee. The white T-shirt Miki had slept in was wrinkled, and her usually crisp green uniform pants were creased in all the wrong places.

"Would you like some fresh clothes?" Christina gripped the counter as if uncertain she should let go.

"No, I'm fine really. If you're all right I need to go home."

Christina looked at her for the first time. "I'm angry."

"That's good, Christina. Stay angry," Miki said softly. "I am going to catch him. I promise you."

Christina's eyes were trusting and dark. Miki felt herself being pulled into their charcoal depths. She swallowed and stepped back.

"Well, Ranger," Christina said, evidently confused by the tension between them. "Bacon, eggs, hash browns," she said distractedly.

"Wait. I can't eat all that. But if you don't mind, I know two deputies who were outside in the cold last night, and I'm sure they would love a trucker's special."

"Good. You invite them in, and I'll go put some clothes on. When I come down, I promise you the best breakfast you ever ate."

Miki watched the teasing tug of her mouth. She was relieved. She thought about the loneliness she'd felt while waiting for sleep to overtake her the night before, the loneliness that would return if Christina decided to go back to Boston.

Chapter Ten

Miki called Kristan's office and got her answering machine. "Kristan, it's Miki. It's"—Miki frowned at her watch— "eleven a.m., and I need a favor. I'll be in town around noon."

If Kristan was off on a news story, she might not get the message until later, but Miki hoped her friend would check her machine before noon.

Miki showered, put on fresh clothes and climbed into her pickup. Her joints and muscles were stiff from her night on the floor. When she left, Christina was frantically cleaning up after breakfast. Then she announced she'd rather cook that night and was pulling out pans. She insisted Miki cancel their reservations. She also insisted she could go to the sheriff's office alone to make a statement. Miki realized it was her way of dealing with the night before.

❧

"I'm glad you're here." Miki said, her hand on the door of Kristan's office.

Kristan jumped up and went to her friend. "Where have you been? I've been looking for you." There was an edge in Kristan's voice.

"You heard?" Miki grinned. "Of course you heard. There isn't much goes on here you don't hear. As for me, a bruised professional ego, but otherwise all right." Miki sighed. "No it's more than that. I'm really angry. I don't know what I would have done if she'd been hurt."

"But she wasn't."

"Luck, Kristan, that's all it was." Miki paced about. "I need a favor."

"Name it."

"A news story, about last night's break-in. I think it'll get Christina the kind of sympathy she needs."

"Actually, I was over at the sheriff's office when you called earlier. I have the police report and just need you to fill in the blanks. This isn't a favor; I'd do it anyway." Kristan reached for her pen and reporter's notebook. "We don't have home invasions around here, and a woman alone . . . Well, by the time I'm done I'll have the whole community looking for the jerk." Kristan looked up expectantly, her pen poised over the notebook. "What time did you get there?"

"Around one a.m.," Miki said, and proceeded to relay the details.

The interview was over in minutes. "I'd like to talk with Christina, to get her reaction."

"That wouldn't be a very good idea," Miki hedged.

"Why not? I'll just give her a call."

"She's a very private person." Miki hoped that would dissuade her, especially if she was on deadline.

Kristan sat back in her chair and studied her "You want to tell me what's going on?"

Miki shifted in her chair. "Nothing is going on." She sounded defensive, even to her own ears.

"Uh-huh."

"I mean it."

"Uh-huh."

"Really." Miki jumped up and went to the window. Kristan crossed her arms and waited. "Last night when dispatch called and told me what had happened, I could hardly breathe. I drove . . ." Miki gulped. "I am not even going to tell you what speeds I drove to get here. And then when Christina was in my arms crying, it turned my world upside down." Miki paused as she tried to put words on what had been so illusive before, buried in the emotions deep inside. "I am so angry at myself," she finally said. "She was vulnerable, scared and I wanted to crush her against my body. I wanted to kiss her, for God's sake. I don't even want to think about what might have happened if Scott and Peter hadn't been there. I would've probably acted like a damn predator."

"You've fallen in love," Kristan said with a big grin.

"No, no, no, no." Miki's fist came down on a pile of folders Kristan had on her bookcase. The folders jumped like a diver off a springboard and cascaded to the floor. Miki bent over to pick them up, and she felt some of the anger dissolve in the mindless act of putting the papers back in the folders. "I'm sorry," Miki said, embarrassed.

"Don't worry about it. Those are just old files."

"I like her, that's all," she said as much to convince Kristan as to convince herself.

"No, Mik, what you have is terminal, it's called . . . love," she said seriously.

Miki finished replacing the files and sat back down. Kristan was silent, watching her, and Miki finally blurted, "I am," relieved to articulate what had been whirling in her mind.

Kristan went over and took Miki's hand

"I want to be with her all the time. And when I'm not with her, I'm thinking about her. I make up excuses to be with her. Sometimes I look at her and I can't even breathe. I'm afraid of what I am feeling." Miki searched Kristan's face, wishing for some key to explain this. "What really worries me is that the longer you're with someone, the harder it is to leave. Does that make sense?"

"Absolutely. That's what happened when I met Jennifer. I was an emotional stew, everything jumbled in one big pot. I loved her, then I hated her because I thought she didn't love me. I wanted to be with her every moment yet preserve some distance. Getting a handle on all of those emotions was like trying to herd rabbits." Kristan chuckled. "Now we are joined. It's as though we were two halves of a whole going through a parallel universe. We think alike, feel passionate about the same things—it's weird."

Frustrated, Miki pulled away from Kristan and stuffed her hands in her pockets, her long legs stretched out in front of her, her feet hidden under Kristan's desk. "I've got to solve this case and get away from here."

"Have you indicated to . . ."

"God no. She doesn't have a clue."

"How does she feel?"

"Like any straight woman—grateful."

"Grateful?"

"Grateful that I believed her when no one else around here would. Grateful that I'm here to help her. Although . . ." Miki shrugged.

"You feel you blew it by leaving for Jackman with no one there to watch over her."

"Yeah, big time." Irritated, Miki pushed a hand through her hair.

"Someone figured that out."

Miki scowled at Kristan. "You heard? Of course, everyone heard I had the place under surveillance." Miki sighed. "This case has a skunky smell. Pranks are one thing. At first I thought it was just kids listening to their parents and acting out their frustrations because she was giving them a hard time crossing her land. But the guy who tried to break in was an adult, and he had a gun. There's something here I'm missing."

"But what?"

Miki raised her eyebrows and stared hard at Kristan. She had slipped into her cop mode. "I haven't figured that out yet. I think last night our perpetrator just went one step further. I think whoever is doing this started out to scare her, but last night he crossed over the line."

"That's the angle I plan to use in my story. That harmless pranks have turned into a real horror for a Boston woman."

"I love it," she smiled.

"What's next?"

"More surveillance. Then some kind of trick to catch the guy." Miki stood up, buttoned her jacket and put on her hat. "Tell Jennifer to warm up her yellow pad; she's going to be prosecuting this buzzard in the not-too-distant future."

"Where you going?"

"I've work to do."

"Lunch?"

"Another time." Miki had her hand on the door, ready to leave.

Kristan laughed. "Would you hold on?"

Miki stopped.

"Mik, you've got to resolve that other issue. You can't bury it under a mound of work and pretend it isn't there."

"I can't confront it. I'd be unprofessional."

"You have to."

"No, Kristan. What I have to do is ignore it." Miki didn't care if she sounded petulant. Any inappropriate behavior from her and she'd lose Christina's trust.

Kristan threw up her hands in capitulation. She knew better than to argue any further. "Okay, but I'm here if you need to talk."

Miki's face softened. "I know." She started out the door again.

"Would you hold on? God, you remind me of a whirling dervish. I'm trying to coordinate your schedule with ours so we can have dinner again. So."

"So, what?"

"So when will you be free for dinner?" She knew Miki didn't

mean to be difficult; she just didn't want to be pinned down. "How about in a couple of days."

"Bring Christina if you'd like."

"Ah. Not a good idea." Miki frowned, afraid of how Christina would react to her gay friends and uncertain about how Christina would respond to the part of her life that defined who she really was. "Look I'm just not ready to deal with a whole lot of things. Okay?"

"Okay," Kristan said, shaking her head.

Miki finished her paperwork and asked the dispatcher to run a motor vehicle check on Billy Clark; she had remembered the number on his license plate. She also asked them to run his name through NCIC. If he had a criminal record, they would have it. He might feel justified in pushing the issue, Miki thought, because Billy was simple enough to believe he had some claim to that land.

After she left the sheriff's office, Miki went back to her cabin. After a shower and a change of clothes, she was at Christina's house by seven. She frowned when she saw the other cars in the driveway. She thought they'd be having a quiet dinner for two.

"Come in, come in," Christina enthused as she pulled Miki by the arm. "I started cooking, and it just got out of hand. I thought, it's New Year's Eve, what a great time to get to know some people. So when I was at the sheriff's office this morning, I invited everyone."

Miki glanced around. Scott was standing near the fireplace, drinking champagne. He was dressed in dark blue slacks and a blue and white rugby shirt. Peter and his wife, Carol, were on the sofa. He waved to her; she smiled at him. Janey came over and gave Miki a hug. At first she was thrown by the unexpected situation, but she quickly adjusted and hugged Janey back.

"Janey has been telling high school stories," Christina said as she poured her a glass of champagne.

"I've been telling tales about you." Janey stopped when she saw

Miki's look of displeasure. "Only the good stuff, like the time you and Kristan locked the French teacher in the supply closet."

Miki groaned.

"Don't worry I told them how mean she was." Janey was laughing. "It was wild. She was in there for an hour pounding and hollering. The janitor had to let her out. The next day the principal came to our classroom because there were too many of us to call into his office. We had all sworn an oath we wouldn't squeal, then Bruce Chambers, that wimpy little guy, ratted on Miki and Kristan. I thought Mrs. LaBroue was going to have a heart attack." Janey turned to the others. "Kristan and Miki were her best students."

"What happened?" Carol asked.

"We were suspended." Miki grinned as she remembered those days. "Spent the whole week fishing, right here on Chandler Lake."

Christina was laughing. "A bit of a lawbreaker?"

"Just a bit." Miki looked at Janey. "No more stories, or I'll tell some about you," she threatened good-naturedly. "Like the time you—"

"I give up. I promise, no more stories." Janey laughed as she held up her hands in mock surrender.

"Where's Harold?" Miki asked.

"He wanted to baby-sit. He hates New year's eve parties."

Peter told the group stories about some of the pranks his two teenage boys had pulled, and Janey joined in with stories about her two youngsters. Christina moved about the room making sure glasses were filled, hors d'oeuvres eaten. She joined in the conversation each time she returned from the kitchen. Miki laughed with the rest, but she kept an eye on Scott, who was watching Christina.

"You're not from around here," Miki said to Scott during a lull in the conversation.

"Nope. Moved here from Connecticut about six years ago."

"Scott was married to Shirley Peterson—you know, the Petersons from over in Bayport." Peter stopped when he realized what he was saying.

"It's okay. Everyone knows we're separated," Scott said.

Christina stepped into the uncomfortable silence. "Well, dinner is ready." She linked arms with Janey and Miki. "Let's go into the dining room."

The table was decorated with streamers and noisemakers. Candles were lit. "Peter you and Carol sit here." Christina gestured to her left. "Scott, why don't you sit to my right. Janey, you can sit next to Scott, and Miki, please sit there." Christina gestured to the head of the table. Christina poured the wine, then sat down at the other end.

Miki took her place and looked across the table. Christina smiled at her, her face a soft glow in the candlelight. Miki stared. Kristan was right—she was breathtakingly beautiful.

Scott said something to Christina, and she turned to talk with him as she passed the dishes around. Given the number of dishes on the table, Miki realized Christina must have been cooking all day long.

Peter lifted his glass. "I'd like to propose a New Year's toast," he offered. "To new friends"—he gestured to Christina—"and old friends. And to family." He gently clinked his glass against his wives. The rest also clinked their glasses.

"Thank you." Christina clinked her glass against Peter's and Scott's and acknowledged the others. As she sipped her wine, she looked at Miki.

Miki held her breath. She was beginning to feel warm again. "I beg your pardon?" Miki had not heard what Janey had said to her.

"You were a million miles away. I said, Christina looks relaxed."

"Yes, yes she does."

For the rest of the meal, Miki talked with Janey and Carol. When she looked up she would catch Christina just looking away from her. She tried to hear what she, Peter and Scott were talking about, but Janey and Carol kept up their own chatter. She did notice that Peter was doing most of the talking and that Christina was laughing.

"This is wonderful," Janey said to Christina as she tasted more of the broiled haddock swimming in a creamy lobster and shrimp sauce. "I wish I could cook like this. These flavors are wonderful together."

"Thank you." Christina was clearly pleased.

"I couldn't get away with anything this exotic with my kids. They're strictly hamburger and chicken," Janey said. "Harold promised them pizza tonight. They were so excited."

"I used to experiment every now and then," Carol joined in, "when my kids were growing up, but Peter was always a meat-and-potatoes man, and there wasn't much room for creativity."

"Good stick-to-your-ribs food," Peter said.

Carol smiled at her husband's remark. "But I agree with Janey. This is wonderful and a wonderful break from meat and potatoes."

"Do you plan to stay here?" Scott's question to Christina was loud enough so that everyone stopped to listen.

"That depends"—Christina hesitated and looked over at Miki— "on whether my friend over there can catch the bad guy. I find I'm liking it here more and more," she added softly.

"We'll catch him," Scott said before Miki could answer. "In fact, I was talking to the sheriff just today. There might be some leads."

"Really?" Christina looked over at Miki.

Miki didn't say a word; she was watching Scott.

Scott cleared his throat and looked over at the sheriff. "We checked on the whereabouts of some people who we know have criminal records. We ran some background checks on some others."

"That's not to say," Peter added hastily, "they are suspects, but there are a couple of guys around here who are capable of harassing someone like this."

"Get anything?" Miki asked, clearly feeling out of the loop.

"Some possible things to look into," Peter said.

"Well, I hope you catch him," Janey said. "I want Christina to stay." She smiled at her hostess.

"Thank you," Christina said.

"We'll catch him," Scott postured. "I have several feelers out in the community, people who only talk to me. There are no secrets here, someone always knows something."

Miki looked down at her plate. She wanted to be somewhere else. She heard Scott say something to Christina, and the conversation split again between the two ends of the table. Carol and Janey talked about a new program at the school that allowed parents to sit in the class and watch their children at work.

Miki occasionally peeked at her watch. It was only ten, and she couldn't bear the thought of waiting for midnight. She fingered her pager, wishing it would go off and give her an excuse to use the telephone, or even an excuse for leaving. In Jackman, she could be certain the pager would beep, but not here; the colonel had told her to focus on this case. She looked around. Everyone had finished eating.

"Why don't we have coffee and dessert in the living room?" Christina rose and picked up a tray with a coffee server and cups on it, which Scott took from her. He gave her his big megawatt smile. Miki followed them from the table. She hated smiles like that and decided she wanted to go home.

"Ah, Christina," she said, hesitating. "I'd love coffee and dessert, but I really need to make a few calls. So I should be going." She looked at her watch as if time was critical to making those telephone calls.

"Nonsense, you can use my office." Christina turned to the others. "This will take just a minute. Scott, set the coffee there." She pointed at the table near the sofa. "Carol, if you would pour, I'll get Miki settled in my office and then get the dessert."

Before Miki could respond, Christina had her by the arm, the heat of her touch sizzling.

"This is wonderful," Christina said as she walked Miki through the hallway to another room. "I felt nervous and uncomfortable at first, but I think everyone is having a good time. Even Scott seems genuinely concerned." When Miki didn't respond, Christina turned to her. "Is everything okay?"

"Sure, I just need to make those calls." Her response was clipped.

"Well have at it," Christina smiled. "Thanks for being here." In an awkward moment Christina tried to put her arms around Miki's neck to give her a hug, then settled for sliding them around her waist and giving her a squeeze. Just as quickly she left, quietly closing the door behind her.

I've turned into a zombie. Miki stared at the closed door. The woman simply wanted to hug me in that familiar straightway women do, and I was afraid to raise my arms to respond. She sat down at the desk. She rested her head in her hands. She picked up the telephone, called Kristan and asked her if she could come over.

"Come over. We both hate going out on New Year's Eve, so we decided on a quiet night at home," she said.

"Oh, wow, I don't want to get in the middle of a romantic night."

"Miki, you're my best friend, but sometimes you are—" Kristan stopped. "Just come over. Jennifer and I would love to see you."

"Thank you."

They hung up. On the wall were pictures of Christina in various stages of life. She was even beautiful as a child, Miki thought. There were framed photos of Christina on skis, at the beach. And several of Christina as a teenager.

Miki could hear the slow buzz of conversation. "Christina," Miki paused as everyone turned to look at her. "I have to go."

"So soon?" Miki noted Christina's disappointment.

"Yes, a friend of mine isn't feeling well. I promised I would check on her." Miki suppressed an inward shudder. The excuse sounded lame, even to her. "Anyway, Happy New Year, everyone. And thank you, Christina."

Later that evening, Miki sat on her bed. She still regretted the look of disappointment on Christina's face when she told her she had to go. She, Kristan and Jennifer talked for hours, but she didn't get any closer to resolving her dilemma than she had been earlier.

Miki turned off the light. She was going to have to spend more time on the case and less time with Christina. She also had to catch a criminal, a man she was beginning to hate. She also hated the disorganization that was overtaking her life and the unbridled emotions that seemed to have a life of their own. Stick with the investigation, she told herself as she drifted off to sleep.

Chapter Eleven

Miki wanted to ignore the ringing telephone, but it kept pulling her away from a warm and fuzzy dream. She wanted to hold on to the dream, not let it escape. She was groggy when she answered, but sat up in bed when she heard Christina's voice. "Is something wrong?"

"No." Christina's laugh was warm, comforting. Miki frowned; it reminded her of her illusive dream. "I should have realized you'd switch to your cop mode. No, nothing is wrong, and I'm sorry I woke you. I was going to invite you to go cross-country skiing with me. I thought it might be nice to look at the property together. Ski down to the lake. Maybe talk about some ways to resolve this public access dilemma."

Miki agreed, and one hour later she pulled into Christina's driveway. The woman was standing next to the shed, her skis resting casually against her shoulder.

Miki reached into the bed of the truck and pulled out her skis, swung them over her shoulder and said, "Happy New Year."

"And Happy New Year to you. You're prompt." Christina picked up her knapsack. She started to put her arms through the straps.

"Why don't you let me carry that." Miki reached for the bag.

"I'm puny, Ranger, but not that puny."

Miki blushed. "I didn't mean that." She stopped and scratched her head. "I . . ."

"And I'm teasing you." Christina's face was open, her eyes midnight black in the afternoon sun. "Here, you can carry it."

They strapped on their skis and were companionably quiet as they followed the trail.

"How long have you been with the ranger service?"

"More than a decade. After I graduated from college, I attended classes at the academy in Waterville. When I graduated I was assigned to the Jackman region, and I've been there ever since."

"Do you like being a ranger?"

Miki concentrated on the swishing sound of their skis as she thought about Christina's question. "Most of the time."

"What don't you like?"

"Not winning."

"And you feel you're not winning here?"

"Something like that." Miki slowed down. Christina stopped just ahead of her. "You don't like questions."

"I'm frustrated." Miki said quietly.

"You need to split some wood." Christina teased.

"You're right." Miki grinned. She started moving again, comforted by the rhythm of the skis. Christina stayed even with her as they skied down Bang's Hill.

Chandler Lake lay in the distance. Miki looked for ice fishermen, but the lake looked deserted. She was glad because she would have been reluctant to intercede if Christina was in a mood to throw people off the lake. She wanted to find a compromise, and forcibly removing someone from the ice would only make the locals more entrenched.

Christina stopped near some birch trees, their limbs bare of leaves, and their tall trunks as white as the snow around them. "I used to come here with my grandfather," she said quietly. "It never changes."

Miki took in the panoramic view. The lake was so large, you couldn't see to the other side. What now was covered with ice was a military blue in the summer. Snow-covered trees and bushes lined the shore.

"Relieved?" Christina nodded toward the empty lake.

Miki grinned. "Somewhat."

"Don't worry. I wasn't going to confront anyone. I thought it might be nice, though, to just talk." Christina unsnapped her skis. She reached for the pack on Miki's back. Miki slipped her arms out of the straps and handed the pack to Christina. "Hungry?"

"A little."

Christina walked to the edge of the lake and brushed snow from a large rock. "Your table awaits you," she said formally.

Miki bowed just as formally, "Thank you, madam. May I assist you to your chair?" Miki held out her hand.

Christina slipped her hand into Miki's. "Thank you." Miki helped her climb onto the rock. She sat cross-legged looking at the lake. Miki crawled up next to her on the rock. "Beautiful," Christina breathed.

"Yes, it is."

"I come here every day. Not necessarily to this spot, but to the lake. It's a magnet of solitude, and I feel spiritually at peace here." Christina looked at Miki. "Does that sound silly?"

"No. Not at all." Miki watched an eagle circle overhead. She pointed. "Look!"

"Wow. Do you think it lives around here?"

Miki shaded her eyes with her hand. "Probably. She's an adult. Her mate's probably not far away."

"How do you know she has a mate?"

"Eagles are monogamous; they mate for life."

"Unlike people."

"Unlike people," Miki murmured. She watched as the eagle soared deeper into the woods, finally disappearing.

Christina reached into the backpack. "Coffee?"

"Thanks."

"I've asked about you."

Miki looked into Christina's eyes.

"You're not only the youngest sergeant in the agency, you're the only woman sergeant in the state."

"Just luck."

"I doubt that. I expect that quiet personality of yours has fooled more than one bad guy."

Miki thought about Christina's assessment. "Possibly."

Christina laughed. "You really are uncomfortable talking about yourself." Christina's gaze never wavered.

Miki smiled. "I am. But what about you?"

Christina dug into the pack and pulled out several containers. "I thought you'd heard enough about me that day at your cabin, but ask away, Sergeant." She lifted up the lids and then handed Miki a plate and silverware wrapped in a linen napkin.

"This is quite a picnic. Linen napkins and all. Nice. Thank you."

Christina pointed at the containers. "Pâté, salmon almondine and rice pilaf."

Miki sighed. "Thank God you packed lunch. Mine would have been tuna sandwiches and potato chips."

"I love to cook, and this gave me a good excuse." Christina handed her a serving spoon, and they helped themselves. Then Christina leaned back against the rock, her plate balanced comfortably on her knees. "Questions?"

"Actually, I'm not certain that I have a need to know. Really, your personal life is not part of the investigation."

"But is it a part of getting to know someone?"

"Yes." Miki stared at the steam twirling from her plate. She tasted the salmon first. "This is great."

"Thank you." Christina was pleased.

"All right, have you lived in Boston your whole life?" Miki realized she was even more curious about Christina.

"Mostly, except for the years I spent at Yale. After I graduated I immediately went to work for my father, met ex-husband, married and now separated, permanently I might add." Miki heard the determination in Christina's voice.

"Will he be joining you up here? You mentioned you remained friends." Miki found she was holding her breath even as she asked the question. She was surprised at her reaction.

"No." Christina stopped. "I am forty years old and I just needed some place to sit and think. This is my space." Christina looked expectantly at Miki. "Eventually, I want to go back into advertising if I return to Boston, but for a while, I just want to hide out, listen to the birds and watch it snow." Christina looked boldly at Miki. "Now it's your turn."

"I didn't realize we were taking turns."

"Well, we are."

"What do you want to know?"

"Where were you born?"

"Here in Bailey's Cove. I went to school here and then college at the University of Maine. After I graduated, like I said before, I went to the academy, graduated, I've been a ranger ever since. I'm forty-two years old."

"You like it."

"Yeah, I do."

"I bet you like the investigative part."

"I do. It's like putting a giant puzzle together. Each piece has its place, and no one segment is more important than any other. And then there's the aha factor."

"Aha?"

Miki's felt puckish. "You know. The light bulb goes on, the cobwebs clear, and all of a sudden you go 'Aha, I found the answer.'"

Christina laughed with Miki. "I like that."

Miki felt uncomfortable with Christina's gaze on her. "This tastes wonderful."

"Thank you. It has been fun cooking again."

Miki set her dish down next to her and looked out across the lake. "But we're here to talk about the lake and trying to resolve an access problem."

"You're very good at that."

"At?"

"Switching topics when you don't want to talk about something."

"But we're here to talk about the lake."

Christina sighed. "Right. I guess I don't understand why everyone has gotten so excited. There are roads that lead to the lake. I don't understand why people insist on going across my property and now lay claim to it. Scott told me what that man said. Claims my grandfather promised ten acres to his grandfather. I doubt that."

"I doubt it also, but Billy is—well, let's just say a little different. I think I can reason with him. But the larger picture is public access. True, there are roads, but for people on this side of the lake, it's a twenty-minute drive. Look, Christina, I know people are trespassing on your property, but the problem started years ago. I can remember my grandfather bringing me here as a kid, right across your property. Your grandfather allowed it, and your dad wasn't around all that much to stop it. Granted, in your grandfather's day there were fewer people, but the fact is people have gotten used to using your land."

"But now that I'm here, why can't they respect my privacy? I wouldn't think of going into someone else's yard just to take a shortcut."

"Well, that's city thinking."

"City thinking?"

"In the city, people are extremely territorial. They put up fences, real or symbolic, and everyone else abides by them. People in cities walk on sidewalks; they don't cut across lawns. It's different here. There are no fences. Look around you. People just live next to one another without barriers. So when someone comes along and puts up no trespassing signs, they react. I'm not saying it's right, I am just saying it is."

Christina sat quietly looking at the lake. "I didn't come here to start a war, I just came here to find something I lost a long time ago."

When she didn't continue, Miki said softly, "It's difficult. You have a right to privacy, and you own the land that should dictate that privacy. But it's going to be impossible to change patterns that have existed for decades."

"Decades?"

"Decades," Miki said matter-of-factly.

"Have you come up with a solution?"

"Yes, but I don't think you're going to like it."

"Try me."

"Deed a right-of-way to the town. A section of land on the farthest tip of your property. Let the town cut a roadway through, and I believe people will use it and leave you alone. I think that's about the only solution."

Miki watched Christina's body language. She unconsciously shifted her weight on the rock, crossed her arms over her chest and sat silently studying the horizon. Miki did not interrupt.

"I'll think about it," she said finally. She rested her chin against her knee. "I won't promise anything."

"I'm not asking for any promises."

"I talked with John. Told him what was happening. About the noises in the night. I didn't tell him about the attempted break-in."

"Why not?"

"He'd insist I move back to Boston. We may not be husband and wife, but he still feels protective." Christina's eyes were expressive as she looked at Miki. "I don't want to go. When I told him that, he offered to come here. But I told him you were protecting me."

Miki forced herself not to react. She felt uncomfortable knowing she had been discussed by Christina and a man she did not know.

"We talked a long time about the possibility of a right-of-way. I figured that was what you were going to suggest. He also thinks that would solve my problems." Christina sighed. "I told him I would think about it. He has much the same opinion of me you have though. Said I was being stubborn." Christina suddenly laughed. "I am."

Miki looked at her watch.

"You have to go?"

"I have an appointment in town this afternoon."

Miki helped Christina pack up.

"One other thing. That man who said my grandfather promised his family some of our land . . . Do you think he might be the one who tried to break into my house?"

"I don't know him. I did run a background check on him, though. With the holidays I haven't gotten the results. Remember he is not very bright. It might have been something he heard as a kid and never forgot."

"I find it difficult to believe my grandfather gave anything away. It wasn't like him, but then being here does strange things to you." Christina's eyes were warm. "I've enjoyed this."

"Me too. I was wondering, would you like to go snowmobiling sometime?"

"I'd love it." Christina stood up and brushed the snow from her ski pants. She slipped off the rock and reached for the backpack. "My turn to carry."

The trip back was comfortably quiet. And when they arrived at Christina's house, Miki was quickly on her way.

Chapter Twelve

Miki scowled at her watch. She had been careful in her conversation at Tippy's, telling just a few that she would be out of town over the weekend, pretending that it had slipped out and then begging an oath of secrecy. She stopped to tell the sheriff about her plan, but Janey said he was at a day-long conference. She wasn't interested in talking to Scott.

She had seen Christina every day since their picnic down by the lake. There were long walks in the woods, followed by coffee in front of the fireplace. Miki found herself thinking more and more about her and Christina. She knew there were land mines, and she knew she couldn't avoid them. She had decided not to tell Christina about her plan to mislead the guy into believing she would be out of town. She didn't want to disappoint her, if her plan did not work.

When she got to the shed on Friday night, a fresh pot of coffee and sandwiches were waiting for her. It had become a ritual that Miki looked forward to.

As the clock ticked toward midnight, though, she began to doubt her plan. Sitting in the dark, she sipped her third cup of coffee and wondered if she should bag it and come back the next night. Suddenly there was movement beside the house. Miki quietly set her coffee on the table. There had been just a shadow, so she waited and watched. Again she saw a shadow alongside the house. She zipped up her snowmobile suit, pulled her hood up around her head and eased the door open.

She circled behind the shed and waited, breathing into her snowmobile suit so the vapor from her breath wouldn't give her away. Then a figure stepped clear of the shadows. He was dressed in black with a black ski mask over his face. He stopped at the window Christina had repaired.

Miki unhooked the snap on her holster. She crouched down and crept toward the figure. She had always been reluctant to use a gun. In her years as a ranger, it had been out of her holster only once, and that was when she couldn't calm down a poacher twice her size who was determined to get away.

The intruder was smaller than her. With his back to her, he was just reaching up to the window when Miki saw the crowbar.

"Stop right there. Police," Miki ordered.

He whirled around and raised his arm. Miki ducked to her right, but the crowbar connected with the side of her face. She grabbed the man by his collar and pushed his arm down, putting just enough pressure on his wrist to make him drop the weapon. All her years of working out paid off, she thought. He dropped the crowbar in the snow, and, with her feet planted firmly on the ground, she used her leg to upend him. He went down on his back with a loud thump, and Miki put her knee in his chest. He started yelling for help, his pleas muffled by the ski mask. She saw the terror in his eyes.

Miki reached to her belt and grabbed her handcuffs. Ordinarily she would roll him over, but he was strong and he was struggling, and she didn't want to take the pressure of her knee off his chest.

She snapped the handcuff on the wrist she was holding. The man kept trying to hit her with his other hand.

When she yanked on the handcuff, he let out another yelp as the steel cut into his wrist. Miki grabbed his other arm, pulled it across her knee and snapped the handcuff on. She stood up to catch her breath and felt the blood on the side of her cheek. There was pain just below her ear where the crowbar had connected, and the blood seeped into her mouth. Miki saw the light go on in the upstairs bedroom.

She patted him down and found what she was looking for. With a ballpoint pen, she eased the .22 caliber pistol out of his jacket pocket.

Suddenly, the outside floodlight went on.

"Are you all right?" Christina rushed out the front door and was rounding the side of her house when Miki pulled the man to his feet. She stopped and stared at the gun dangling from Miki ballpoint.

"I wasn't doin' nothin'," he whined.

"Call the sheriff's department," Miki said.

Christina, who had thrown a jacket over her nightgown, came toward her. "You're bleeding." Miki touched the side of her face with her hand. She could feel the jagged edge of the cut just below her ear. Blood was already coagulating in the cold.

"Not badly, Mrs. Reynolds. Please just go in the house and call the sheriff."

When Christina turned toward the door, Miki set down the gun and yanked the ski mask off Clark's face, pulling hair with it.

He yelped like a wounded bear. "I wasn't doin' nothin'."

"Tell that to the sheriff." She grabbed him by the collar again. "Well, Billy Clark, you are in trouble for breaking and entering— I suspect, your second attempt?" Miki read the worry in his eyes. She touched the blood on the side of her face. "Assaulting an offi- cer. Oh yeah, I need to read you your rights. You have the right to remain silent . . ."

When Christina returned, she had a first-aid kit in her hand. "I called the sheriff's department. They said the sheriff and a deputy would be here in a few minutes." Christina studied Miki's face again. "It looks deep. Why don't you at least come inside and I can look at it."

"I'd rather keep Mr. Clark out here."

"All right, then at least bend down so I can wipe that cut with an antiseptic pad." Christina gently took Miki's face in her hand, and Miki swallowed hard as she bathed in the comfort Christina offered her. She had difficulty staying focused.

"Just a second," she told Christina. She grabbed Billy Clark by the neck. "On your knees and face the house," she ordered. Christina's fingers were warm against the side of her face as she pushed her hair back to study the cut. "It might need stitches."

Miki kept an eye on Clark, who was slumping lower and lower. Then she saw the blue lights through the trees. She was surprised that they hadn't used their sirens. Boy cops loved running with lights and sirens.

Miki stepped back from Christina. "I'll be fine." She heard the car doors slam.

Although Christina frowned, she didn't say anything.

"What we got here?" the sheriff asked as he approached Miki. Scott and several other deputies followed close behind him.

"Caught him trying to break into Mrs. Reynold's." Miki held the gun out in front of her. "Found this."

"Get me an evidence bag from the cruiser," Peter said to one of his deputies.

"I wasn't doin' nothin'."

"You okay, Miki?" Peter eyed the bloody antiseptic pads in Christina's hand.

"Fine. Why don't you take him to your office. I'll question him there." Miki nodded toward Clark. "I'll be there in a minute. I have to get my truck."

"Scott could give you a ride," the sheriff offered.

"I'll do it," Christina said.

"Mrs. Reynolds, really . . ." Miki began.

"Don't argue. I have my car here, and I'm not going to get much sleep tonight. Let me just go in and change."

Miki noted Scott's hyperthyroid look as he ogled Christina's blue silk nightgown, its hem slightly wet from the snow, then gazed up to where her jacket had opened and exposed the deep neckline of the gown just above her breasts. Miki felt a flash of jealousy.

"Okay. Just go change, please," Miki said sternly.

Christina gave Miki a puzzled frown as if uncertain why she snapped. Without another word, she went into the house.

"Put him in the car," Peter said to Scott. Scott grabbed Clark by the shoulder and pushed him forward. Peter called to another of his deputies, "You ride with him."

Scott said, "I can take him in, Sheriff."

"I want Jerry to ride with you." A scowl briefly crossed Scott's face and then disappeared. "You drive," Scott told the other deputy.

Peter watched the two men walk toward Scott's cruiser. "You know he'll make bail before you even have your paperwork done."

"I know."

"At most you got an attempted B and E, assaulting an officer. Betcha the judge sets bail at five hundred bucks."

"Wouldn't surprise me. He has a record, NCIC gave me that when I ran a check on him after the holidays. But nothing serious. It'd be nice if he had been some kind of ax murderer, it would up the bail." Miki dabbed at the cut on the side of her face with the antiseptic pads Christina had given her. Blood continued to run down her cheek and into her collar.

"This the same guy Scott told me about? Claims ownership of some of Mrs. Reynold's land?"

"Same one. He should have waited. Christina and I talked about it. At first she dismissed it, but later said she would think about it." Miki paused. "By the way, Peter, I did call your office today to tell you about tonight's surveillance."

"I figured you had. I was at a day-long training session in Waterville," he offered. "Sorry I wasn't here, but it looks like you handled it just fine." Peter turned when Christina came out.

"I think she should go to the hospital," Christina said to the sheriff.

"Is it bad?"

"Just a cut. I'll stop by the emergency room after we book him," Miki said. She gave Christina a look that told her not to argue.

Christina reached into her pocket and pulled out her keys. "My car is in the garage."

"I'll see you at the station," Peter said. "We'll run a check on that gun, see if it's stolen."

"Here." Christina handed Miki more antiseptic pads. "If you won't let me take you to the emergency room, at least hold these against the side of your face to stop the bleeding."

"Wouldn't want to get blood on your seats."

"They're leather. It won't hurt them." Christina was clearly hurt by Miki's comment. "I was thinking more about your discomfort."

Miki could feel the adrenaline that had flowed drain from her. "I'm sorry, you're right." She took the gauze pads. "Thank you."

"Will he go to jail for a long time?" Christina asked as she started her black Mercedes. The powerful engine rumbled alive.

"I don't know. It depends on the judge, but the D.A. is a friend of mine, so I don't think she'll let him cop a plea. But we're not talking years in jail, maybe only weeks, possibly only days."

"So my problems aren't over."

"More than likely they are. I think being caught will scare him enough to leave you alone."

They rode in silence the rest of the way. The wound on the side of Miki's face was throbbing. When they reached the sheriff's department, Miki tried to persuade Christina to go home, but she insisted that she wanted to wait and take Miki back to her snow-mobile.

After reading him his Miranda rights for a second time, Miki questioned Clark for more than an hour, more time than she ordinarily would have spent on an attempted break and enter. But Clark stuck to his story. He said he was on his way to the lake, but he had no explanation for why he had deviated so far off the path. He said he had struck her with the crowbar because she had frightened him. He denied he had attempted to break into Christina's house in the past.

As she closed the door to the interrogation room, she had a feeling Clark had been coached. But when, she wondered, because he had not been alone with anyone except the deputies and he had not made any telephone calls.

She went to a vacant desk and began to write her report. She saw Christina seated on one of the visitors' seats, reading what was probably an outdated *Time* magazine.

"The gun is his." Peter held up a printout. "Also, it wasn't loaded, but that doesn't really make sense. Why would a guy take an empty gun to a break-in?"

Miki chewed on her bottom lip. "To scare her, not kill her."

"By the way, the bail bondsman is here," Peter said.

"How much?"

"Five hundred."

"You were right on the money."

"Yeah, ain't justice great," Peter said cynically. "Why don't you get Mrs. Reynolds out of here. I'll take care of the rest of this."

Miki sighed, overwhelmed by exhaustion. "Okay. I'll be back in the morning to finish my paperwork."

"Mik, it's already morning." Peter nodded at the clock.

"Five a.m. I don't believe it."

"Believe it. See you later today, okay?"

"Sure. I'll catch a few hours of sleep, and I'll be in. I have to call my superiors to see what they want me to do next." Miki was especially reluctant to make that call because she'd have to call the colonel at home on a Saturday. She wanted to wrap up the case, but she felt disappointed.

As Miki stepped around the counter, Christina looked up and smiled. "Ready?"

"Ready."

Christina frowned at the hastily applied gauze pad someone at the sheriff's department had taped to the side of Miki's face. Miki knew it was soaked with blood.

"Hospital?" Christina asked.

"If I say no, will I win?"

"Nope."

Miki laughed. "Okay. To the hospital, but just to have it looked at."

The hospital was nearby, and within minutes Christina had parked the Mercedes near an ambulance outside the emergency room.

Miki scowled. The ambulance could delay her if hospital staff was dealing with a real emergency.

"Is that the scowl you reserve for the bad guys?"

"Yes."

"Well, it's not going to work on me."

"Christina, that ambulance means they have a real emergency going on in there, so this might take a while. Why don't you go home?"

"I am going to wait." Her voice was firm. "It's the least I can do."

Miki, her hand on the door, looked Christina in the eyes. "I'm not going to win this argument either, am I?"

"No." Christina smiled. "Shall we go in or would you like to sit out here and freeze to death?"

Miki inhaled. "Okay, but after you drop me off at my snowmobile, you go home to bed. Agreed?"

"Nope."

"What do you mean, nope?"

"I'm going to make you breakfast. It's the least I can do."

"I guess that's another argument I won't win. I know, I know." Miki laughingly held up her hands.

Christina's smile was radiant. "Very astute, Ranger."

"Bit of a stubborn streak there." She gazed deeply into Christina's eyes.

"Very much." Christina's eyes sparkled in the overhead vapor lights.

Miki sat at the same oak table where weeks before she and Christina had shared their first cup of coffee. Christina took bacon and eggs out of the refrigerator and began breakfast.

Only last week, Miki thought, Christina had cooked to avoid how frightened she was of the whole ordeal. Her face had been ragged, her eyes tired that morning. Today, she was ebullient, energetic. Miki felt tired and dirty, and even though she had taken the pain pills the doctor gave her, her head ached. The local anesthetic she got before they stitched her up was wearing off. Her uniform shirt was caked with blood, and she kept pulling it away from where it stuck to her skin.

"Why don't you take that off, and I'll throw it in the wash."

Miki blinked at the suggestion, and she almost choked on her coffee.

"Better yet, go upstairs and take a shower. I can imagine how you must feel—there's probably a tug of war going on between hunger and dirty. Well, you don't need to be either. I'll get you a shirt you can wear." Christina studied Miki's body. "It'll fit."

"Christina," Miki protested. "I think I'll just go home. I can shower there, and I'll stop by later."

Christina put her hands on her hips. "Ranger, the least I can do after you risked your life is wash your shirt and make breakfast for you. Now, take off your shirt. If modesty is an issue . . ." Her voice trailed off as she left the room.

Miki stood up, looking for a way to escape.

"Here," Christina returned to the kitchen and handed Miki a

large wool shirt. Miki looked at it. No doubt it must belong to her husband, she thought. "You can go in there and change. There is an upstairs guest bathroom on the left. Everything is there, extra toothbrushes, whatever you need."

"And if I argue?"

"You'll lose." Christina said softly.

Miki stepped into the pantry, stripped off her shirt and put on the wool shirt. Embarrassed, she handed her shirt to Christina.

"Go." Christina gently pushed her. "Take a shower."

Once in the shower Miki closed her eyes. She was really tired. Christina had been right, though. The hot water felt good. And the guest bath contained anything and everything, including new underwear, that she might need.

She let the water roll down her skin, careful to keep it away from the bandage on her left cheek. She thought about Billy Clark. Something wasn't right. He was too much a simpleton to have held so strongly to his story. Something else was going on.

Miki toweled herself down, then brushed her teeth and threw the toothbrush away. She looked at the various sizes of underpants sitting in their original wrappers on the counter, selected a pair close to her size and put them on. She started to feel human again.

Miki could smell the bacon cooking as she came downstairs.

"You look human again." Christina handed her a fresh cup of coffee.

Miki was ravenous. She ate everything placed in front of her.

Christina smiled. "You were hungry." Christina leaned back in her chair, her own plate cleaned. "What's next?"

"I'll call my superiors later today. I expect that once I tell them that Clark has been caught they'll want me back in Jackman, probably by Monday."

"So soon?"

"Well, we've caught the guy who seems to have been harassing you."

"Are you certain he's the only one?"

Miki studied her coffee cup. "Christina, I can't be certain of anything. This is the guy that was at the lake, the one who claimed he owned some of your land. There is something very hinky about this case." Miki rubbed her eyes. God, she thought, she was tired. "It's not a question of whether I have doubts. The issue is whether my superiors will share those doubts. Frankly, I expect they will order me back to Jackman because usually the Clarks of the world do act alone." Miki looked up at the clock. It was almost nine a.m. She stood up. "Can I help you with the dishes?"

Christina smiled. "Remember, I have a dishwasher? But thanks. Anyway, will I see you before you go?"

"If you'd like."

"I'd like."

Chapter Thirteen

Miki didn't bother to undress when she returned to her cabin. She just dropped onto the bed and within seconds was sound asleep. She heard a telephone ringing in her dreams but refused to answer it. She surfaced and then fell again into a deep slumber.

The telephone nagged at her again from the deepest corner of her dream, but this time she reached for the phone next to her bed.

"Miki?"

"Colonel?" Miki sat upright.

"Still in bed?"

"Yes, sir. Sorry." The alarm clock read three p.m. Miki shook her head, trying to clear the fog from her head.

"It's okay, Miki, heard about the night you had. Good job."

"Thank you, sir. I was going to call you, but I slept longer than I expected."

"Understood. I talked with the sheriff. He said you got yourself cut."

"Not bad, sir. Just a scratch."

"That's not what the sheriff said."

"You know how these locals exaggerate, sir."

"Well, let's not be too cavalier about it if you're hurt. You might need some time off."

"I'm fine, really. The doc put in a few stitches. Last night I had a head pounder, but I'm fine today, really," she said.

"All right, but I want to know right away if there are any problems. The other reason I called, Miki, is that the governor called me this morning. He was pleased with how you handled the case and he wants you to stay on it."

"Beg your pardon, sir?"

"Well, it appears Mrs. Reynolds called him this morning. She said the issue over access still had to be resolved and that the only one she could really work with was you. Said she felt some kind of compromise could be worked out."

Miki shook her head again. She didn't know if she had heard right. "Thank you, sir, but if she believes a compromise can be worked out, I think the sheriff or one of the county commissioners could resolve that issue. I'm rather anxious to get back."

She stared glumly at her austere surroundings. The cabin was a wonderful place to be in the summer, but she was feeling less and less inclined to remain during the winter. Also, there was Christina. Her dreams were a jumble of Christina—in the kitchen, outside, on skis, in the bedroom.

"It appears not. Seems she trusts only you. So I told the governor that we'd keep you on the case. I want you to resolve this, but I want you back in Jackman soon." Miki heard the unspoken message in the colonel's words.

"Yes, sir."

"Call me in a couple of days with a progress report."

"Yes, sir." Miki heard the click; the colonel never said good-bye.

She swung her legs out of bed and noticed for the first time she still was wearing the shirt Christina had loaned her. She added wood to the fire, stripped down to her underwear and made for the shower.

A little later, the phone rang again.

"Hey, little darlin'." Kristan's voice sounded welcoming.

"Kristan, where are you?" Miki said, shrugging into her robe.

"At the office. Heard about your Wonder Woman exploits. I'm proud of you, but heard you got hurt."

"Hardly Wonder Woman. Just a little encounter." Miki sighed. She always marveled at the communication system that seemed to have a life of its own in a small town.

"That's my pal, tough as beef jerky. Anyway, I'm doing a story, and I need details."

Miki recounted what had happened the night before and downplayed her injury.

"How about supper tonight? Jackie said she wants to look at your wound. You know how docs are," Kristan said after they were finished. "Besides, you've been so busy, you haven't had time to visit with your friends." Miki thought about their mutual friend, Jackie, who had given up a medical practice in Boston to work as a doctor Down East.

"Sure. It looks as though I'm going to be here a while."

"I'm glad, but you don't sound happy about it. What's happened?"

"Seems as though Christina called the governor. She told him I solved the harassment problem. She wants me to stay here to negotiate some kind of settlement between her and the locals." Miki groaned. "Kristan, I'm not a negotiator. I don't know what to do. I suggested a compromise to her—that she give the locals an easement along the border of her property and let the town build a road. It would give her the privacy she wants and give the fishermen access to the lake."

"What was her reaction?"

"None really. She said she would think about it."

Kristan was silent for a long while. "Well, little buddy, I'd say do what you do best."

"And what's that?" Miki demanded.

"Be yourself. You have a quiet way about you that could help get the issue resolved. But maybe she's got the hots for you. You'd better watch out," Kristan teased.

"I should have known better than to expect you to be serious."

"How are things with her anyway?"

"Things are fine." Miki felt impatience creeping up her spine. "Need I remind you she's straight."

"So?"

"Kristan." Miki stopped. "I know you're just trying to get a rise out of me. I have everything under control."

"Okay," Kristan said softly. She knew better than to tease too much. "Dinner at seven."

"I need to go to the gym and work out first. I'll be there right after that. By the way, didn't you promise me that once I got back into town you'd join me? A little weightlifting, some aerobics? Do you good."

"I said that, but I changed my mind. I don't want to look like Arnold Schwarzenegger with breasts."

"And I do?"

"Nope, but you don't have a Germanic side and I do. Sorry, bud, I ain't going to add muscles to anything. Jennifer wouldn't approve." Kristan laughed. "If you want, invite Christina."

Miki paused, "I don't think that'd be a good idea right now."

"Okay, but don't say I wasn't trying to help." Kristan laughed and they rang off.

When the telephone sounded again, Miki answered it impatiently.

"Bad time?" Christina asked.

"No, sorry. I overslept."

"Given the night you had I wouldn't have expected anything else."

"Christina, I understand—"

"That I called the governor," Christina finished for her. "Yes, I did. Are you upset?"

"A little. I'm not a negotiator. I think one of the county commissioners or even the sheriff could do a better job."

"I really would like you to handle it," Christina said, her soft tone inviting. Miki could feel her irritation flow away. "Especially after Scott's call."

Miki tensed. "When did he call?"

"This afternoon. He said that now that the perpetrator had been caught, he'd handle the rest of the case. Said he'd talk to people, tell them to leave me alone. It sounded like something out of a John Wayne movie. He was going to protect me. That's when I called the governor." Christina sounded nervous, as if reluctant to relate the other things she and Scott had talked about.

"What you did was okay," Miki said evenly. "I think he was probably just revving his engines. He's pretty ambitious." Ambitious to get into Christina's bed, she thought.

"You're probably right." Christina paused. "Would you like to have dinner tonight?" she asked.

"I would, but I have a dinner date." Miki frowned. She was making the date with Kristan sound more important than it was.

"Of course." Christina was clearly disappointed.

"Look, I'm having dinner with some friends. Why don't you join us?"

"I . . . don't—" Christina stopped. "I'd like that. I can't explain it, but I just don't want to be alone tonight. I know that sounds silly. Will your friends mind?"

"Actually, Kristan asked me to invite you. She's the reporter who wrote those stories."

Miki arranged to pick Christina up around six-thirty, then called Kristan and suffered the teasing, but Kristan seemed pleased that Christina was joining them.

For the rest of the day Miki was busy. She went back to the sheriff's department and finished up her paperwork. Both the sheriff and Scott were off that weekend, and Miki was glad she could avoid them. She was uncertain if she would punch Scott in the nose or knock the legs out from under him. She wondered at her intense dislike for the man.

Throughout the afternoon she fought to control the mental battle that raged in her head over her impulse to invite Christina to dinner. During weak moments in that mental argument she regretted her decision.

Back in her cabin, Miki showered and put on Levi's and a white blouse. She slipped on her boots and down jacket.

She pondered the situation as she drove to Christina's house. The lights on the first floor glowed—warm, welcoming, sensual in the night. A single light burned in the second-floor master bedroom. Miki was familiar with the room decorated in warm shades of lavender. She had taken it all in the night she had put Christina to bed. She never realized she liked lavender that much.

Miki parked in front of the house and was ready to press the doorbell when the door opened. Christina's long black hair fell loose to her shoulders. Miki swallowed.

"Oh dear, I overdid it." Christina frowned at her dress, a muted winter white circled at the waist with a belt.

"You look great, and it's just fine."

"Honest?" Christina's eyes reflected her concern.

"Honest. You look great. I'm certain someone else there will have on a dress. Um . . ." Miki looked around. "I'll wait in the truck while you get your coat. I have to call my office." Miki knew it was rude to leave her, but she went to the truck and used her cell phone to call Kristan. Jennifer answered. "She's wearing a dress," she said anxiously.

Jennifer laughed. "That's all right."

"But we're going to all have jeans on." Miki felt miserable. "She's going to feel out of place." At that moment Christina was locking the door behind her.

"Don't panic. Everything will be fine," Jennifer said gently. "You'll see when you get here."

Miki hung up just as Christina opened the passenger door. "Let me help you." Miki went around to the passenger side and helped Christina into the truck.

111

"Somehow this seemed easier in pants." Christina laughed.

"I bet truck engineers rarely factor in to their design that passengers may be wearing a dress."

Christina laughed again. "I think you're right."

They sat in silence as Miki pulled out of Christina's driveway and onto the road. Miki appreciated how comfortable she felt with Christina at these moments. She liked the fact that neither of them felt compelled to fill the air with words.

"I hope you rested." Christina studied the long slender bandage on Miki's cheek. "Does it hurt?"

"No, it's fine, really." Miki concentrated on her driving. She told Christina about going back to the sheriff's department to complete her paperwork.

"Was it a lot of work?"

"Just tedious. It's more fun catching the bad guys than filling out the papers about why you think they're bad."

"I hadn't thought about that, but I imagine there's a lot of paperwork in your job." Christina watched as the houses flashed past the moving truck. "I didn't thank you."

"For what?"

"Believing me." Christina's sharp black eyes searched Miki's face. "You know no one else believed me."

"I know. I'm sorry. That's not how police investigations are supposed to work. Something got rather screwy here."

"I think the investigating officer let personal interest get in the way of professional duty."

Miki frowned.

"Scott," Christina added. "He seemed more interested in me than in my problem."

"I expect that happens a lot," Miki said softly.

"It happens, but not as much now that I'm older."

Miki turned into Kristan's driveway. The clouds had cleared, and the full moon rested on the edge of bay like a white beach ball floating on the waves.

"Wow." Christina admired the view. "I bet this is beautiful during the day."

"It's quite spectacular."

Christina looked out across the bay. "I'm glad I'm getting to meet some of your friends. Thank you."

Miki didn't respond as she recalled the tug of war she had been playing earlier in the day.

"Is something wrong?"

"Nope, everything is just fine. Here, let me help you out of the truck."

Jennifer opened the door, her black dress complementing her dark eyes and hair. Hugging her Miki whispered in her ear, "Thank you." Jennifer returned the hug. Miki turned to Christina. "Jennifer, this is Christina Reynolds. Christina, my friend Jennifer Ogden, Jennifer is our local assistant district attorney."

The two women shook hands.

"We're glad you could join us," Jennifer said. Miki felt suddenly proud to be there with Christina, whose eyes were sultry, expressive, tantalizing. Dark liquid eyes that you could lose your soul in, she thought. She glanced at Kristan and saw by her teasing look that she hadn't missed a trick "And this is my friend Kristan Cassidy, the one—"

"—who wrote the articles. I want to thank you." Christina's smile was warm, her lips seductive.

"You're welcome. I'm so glad you could join us. Let me take your coat," Kristan offered.

"And that lady holding the wineglass," Miki continued, "is Jackie Claymont, our local sawbones."

"Sawbones, my arse," Jackie said good-naturedly. "Let me look at that cheek of yours."

"It's nothing," Miki groused.

Christina handed Kristan her coat. "Nothing! It just took four stitches and a whole fistful of painkillers."

Jackie gently eased the bandage aside so she could look at the wound. "Who sewed you up?"

"Dennis."

"He's good. You won't have much of a scar."

"Add it to the one in her eyebrow," Kristan said, heading

113

toward the kitchen. Christina looked up at Miki's eyebrow. Miki blushed. "Did she tell you how she got that one?"

"No."

"Playing Tarzan. Only, the rope she tied to the tree let go and she fell. Hit her face on a lawn chair. Lucky she didn't lose an eye."

"Tarzan?" Christina laughed.

"I was just a kid." Miki felt uncomfortable with the attention.

"Come on." Jennifer hooked her arm through Christina's. "Ignore these two. They were crib mates, so you never know what they're going to talk about. Their mothers were best friends, and they grew up together."

"I'm envious. I don't think I've ever had a friend that long. All my friends moved on to other lives."

"Most people don't," Jennifer agreed.

Christina looked at Jackie. "Were you a member of the group?"

"Well, I was a little older. I had to put up with these two following me around like a couple of puppy dogs."

"Puppy dogs?" Kristan said indignantly. "I would hardly characterize us as puppy dogs. We were never puppy dogs. We were spies, soldiers, but never puppy dogs."

After wine and hors d'oeuvres in the living room, they sat down to dinner. Miki recounted the capture and the night she and Christina spent at the police station. Christina was animated as she relayed her struggle to get Miki to the hospital. They talked about Christina's lake-access problem, and Miki appreciated how restrained her friends were at giving Christina advice. Miki watched Christina closely to gauge her reaction to the other women. For the first time, she saw Kristan and Jennifer through a straight woman's eyes, and she focused on how much they acted like a couple.

If Christina was uncomfortable she gave no indication. Finishing up her coffee, she seemed relaxed and disinclined to leave.

Miki glanced at her watch. "It's midnight. I'm beat."

Jackie looked at her watch. "Me too. I spent all day at the clinic."

Miki went to get their coats.

Christina smiled. "I've really enjoyed myself." She looked at Jennifer. "And thank you for putting on the dress. I know our friend here panicked when she saw how I was dressed."

Miki blanched. "How'd you . . . ?"

Jennifer laughed. "Don't explain," she said to Christina. "Keep her guessing. It will do her good. Besides, it was kind of nice to dress up for a change. That doesn't happen too much around here. It's not culturally cool."

"Well, thank you."

Jennifer and Kristan hugged Miki, and Miki watched as Christina hugged all three of them.

"This has been wonderful. Thank you."

"You're welcome here anytime," Jennifer said warmly.

"I feel that. Thank you."

Christina was quiet during the ride back to her house.

"I like your friends," Christina said finally as they pulled into her driveway.

"They're pretty special." Miki turned off the engine. She got out of the truck. "I want to look around, okay?"

Christina laughed. "Of course."

Miki walked Christina to the door and waited for her to open it. "Will I see you tomorrow?"

"Sure. Would you like to go up to Pike's Hill?"

"Yes, I'd like that."

"Good. I'll pick you up on the snowmobile around eleven?"

"Yes."

"Well then, good night," Miki said softly.

Christina hesitated as if she wanted to say something else, but changed her mind. "Good night."

Miki waited until she heard the lock click on Christina's front door, then got her flashlight from the truck and walked around the house to make certain the windows were secure. Checking the shed where she had spent many hours, she felt a wave of loneliness as she thought about how soon the case would come to an end.

Chapter Fourteen

The next morning, Christina seemed distracted and said little when Miki picked her up. They made good time crossing the bog in the snowmobile, and after about fifteen miles, Miki stopped to offer Christina coffee, whereupon she took the cup and went off to sit on a rock by herself. Miki found the silence unnerving.

They went another five miles when Miki stopped again, concerned that Christina might be cold. All she got was a one-word response: "Fine."

When they finally reached Pike's Hill, Miki revved the engine and felt the pull as the sharp-toothed track dug into the ice. The machine growled as it climbed straight up.

Christina tightened her grip on Miki's waist, no doubt to keep from slipping off. She could feel the shape of Christina's thighs against hers, the shape of her breasts as she held on to her waist. Miki squirmed with desire. She was too damned seductive, Miki thought. They had ridden Miki's snowmobile together many times before, but this was the first time Miki felt so palpably aware of Christina's body. She felt as though an electrode had been attached to her nerves. They felt scrambled and disconnected from her body. *Tell her how you feel*, she thought.

Stupid, her brain argued back. Christina was straight, and she'd never ever given any indication that she wanted anything more than friendship. Was it possible she was confusing Christina's gratitude with something else?

At the top of the hill, Miki said, "We just have to walk past this stand of pines and we'll be there." She picked up her backpack and threw it over her shoulder.

Except for the crunch of their feet on the snow and the occasional snap of a frozen twig, the air was silent. Christina waited as Miki pushed snow off of pine branches and held them so she could step through.

Ordinarily, the exertion of tramping through high snow with the sun on her face made Miki feel elated. Today she felt imprisoned by her snowmobile suit and the silence.

A few more feet and Miki pushed aside the last branches and stepped aside so Christina could absorb the full view of Maine's rugged coastline that contrasted so sharply with the serene wooded hills to their left.

Christina gasped. "This is beautiful. I never realized . . ."

Miki smiled. "It is, isn't it. It's busy in the summer—lots of tourists come up here—but it's perfect now." From Pike's Hill the ocean lay in the distance, a dark intense blue against the white of the snow. Lobster boats, huddling monsters up close, looked like tiny seagulls bobbing on the water. She pointed just to the right of the boats. "Jennifer and Kristan live there." To their left the edge of Chandler Lake was just visible. Behind them were thousands and thousands of acres of snow-covered spruce trees. There was another lake in the distance. "Come on. I have a favorite rock. Are you cold?"

"No, really quite warm, thanks."

Miki led the way, again knocking snow off of the branches so they would not dump their load down Christina's back.

"This is my favorite spot. It has the best view."

"This is gorgeous." Christina did a 360-degree turn, and like a clam at high tide she seemed to open a little.

"I brought some sandwiches along. Would you like more coffee?" Miki asked as she handed Christina a sandwich.

"Yes, thank you." Christina sat on the rock, her back propped against another. She nibbled and then bit into the sandwich. "This is good."

"Didn't think I could cook?" Miki teased. "Well, it's pretty hard to screw up tuna."

"It's been years since I've had a tuna sandwich."

"Well, it's pretty much a staple diet around here. Probably because it's cheap and easy." Miki stamped the snow off her boots. She leaned back against a rock, tilted her face to the sun and closed her eyes.

"I want to ask you something, but I am afraid of how you might react." Christina set the sandwich next to her and sipped on her coffee.

Miki opened her eyes and looked at Christina, knowing that the root of the silence was about to emerge. "Does it have something to do with the investigation?"

"No, it's something someone said to me a few days ago, but last night seemed to bring it into sharper focus."

Miki felt her tension rise, and she braced herself against the rock. Her stomach tightened. Christina's eyes were as dark as a hot fudge sundae.

"Are you—" Christina stopped. "I wasn't going to ask." She shifted on the rock. Miki sensed more discomfort. "And I really don't know why it's bothering me so much."

"Christina," Miki said softly, "just ask."

"Are you a lesbian?" The words seemed to rush out like a torrent.

Miki was nonplussed. "Yes."

"And your friends are, of course."

"Yes."

"Kristan and Jennifer are a couple." Christina's statement did not call for a response. "How long have they been together?"

"Three years."

"And Jackie?"

"Jackie lost her partner to cancer several years ago." Miki scowled. "You said someone told you?"

"Scott. He said your interest in the case was, I believe his words were 'sexually driven.'"

Miki laughed in spite of herself. "Wow, that's a first." She scratched he head. "I can assure you I was driven by my frustration with the case, and not by anything else. But if this is something that—"

"Do you have a . . . a . . ."

"A lover? No." Miki wondered where Christina was going with this.

"Why not?"

The question was brazen, but Miki didn't mind. "Well it just never worked out that way."

"Have there been a lot of women in your life?"

"Not a lot. Some." Miki twisted her napkin, suddenly wary of this line of questioning.

"You don't want to talk about it, do you?"

"Not particularly."

Christina turned to her and said, "You know what upset me the most?"

"I can guess. Look, Christina, if you want me to hand your case over to—"

Christina almost toppled off the rock as she sat forward. "You think I'm reacting because I'm homophobic? Good grief, that's not what I'm upset about."

"I don't understand."

"I'm upset that you didn't trust me." Christina put her hand against her chest. "Upset that we have been together for dinner, skiing, snowmobiling and you couldn't tell me about something that's so important to your life. I kept waiting for you to say something, but you never did. Something this important and . . ." She shook her head, clearly at a loss for words.

"Important, but not overwhelmingly consuming. We're quite invisible here." Miki thought about the times she had wanted to tell Christina, but rejected the idea and she knew why. She was afraid. Terrified that Christina would reject her. "Christina," Miki said gently. "I'm a cop. I don't talk about it for a lot of reasons, but mostly because it's unimportant. The only thing that makes me different than you is who I sleep with. Other than that, everything else is about the same. I don't feel a need to talk about it." She shrugged.

"Doesn't that bother you?"

Exasperated, Miki said, "Yeah. Probably. It seems to be an issue right now."

Christina sipped her coffee. "Would you have told me eventually?"

Miki propped her chin in her hand and rested her elbow on her knee. "Probably not," she said after a long while. "What exactly did Scott tell you?"

"It wasn't very nice."

"It rarely is when it comes from a man like Scott."

"He said I was beautiful and desirable and that you were focused on getting me into bed. He said all queers—" Christina stopped. "That was his word. He said gay women are on an ego trip and believe that after that one night with you, a woman is converted."

Miki couldn't hide the grin. "Funny, men want to believe we're as predatory as they are. Christina—"

"I'm embarrassed," Christina interrupted. She made a face. "I let him dictate the parameters of our discussion."

"Scott was right about one thing. You are beautiful. But I'm not an emotional stalker. As far as I'm concerned, things have to mesh,

121

and physical beauty is really quite incidental to attraction." Miki paused. "And as far as the converting thing goes . . ." Miki shrugged again. "Although few lesbians would admit this, and certainly our literature would condemn any such words as heresy, sex between women can be as big a flop as between a man and a woman."

Christina leaned back on her elbows. She stared intently at Miki. Her blue-black hair peeked out from under her dark blue ski cap. "There's a lot riding on that one moment of intimacy. And you're right, it doesn't always lead to fireworks. Sometimes it's not even a weak sparkle." She smiled at Miki. "Even for you guys?"

"Even for us guys."

"You said a lot of other things have to mesh first. What does that mean?"

"It's hard to put into words. What attracted you to John?"

"He's kind. Really quite gentle when he was focused on me. But don't change the subject. What is it for you? What kind of women are you attracted to?"

Miki stared at Christina a long time. "She has to be real. Someone fun and serious, smart and warm. I don't know. I guess I never thought about types before. It happens or it doesn't."

"I think you're right." Christina spoke so softly that Miki almost couldn't hear her.

"I am surprised at one thing." Miki felt the sweat pooling under her snowmobile suit and reached up and unzipped the top.

"What's that?"

"Well, you're taking this awfully well."

Christina laughed. "What, you think we don't have gays in Boston?"

Now Miki felt embarrassed. "No . . . but that it isn't bothering you."

"Not politically correct."

"Ah. That's right, one must be politically correct," Miki said, betraying her cynicism. "When did Scott tell you?"

"After the night you caught Clark."

"What did you tell him?"

"I said it didn't matter. But after last night with your friends, I felt I had to talk to you about this. It is so much a part of who you are."

Miki stood up and looked out across Passamaquoddy Bay. She already had decided she would not be anywhere near Bailey's Cove this summer. She ignored Christina's enthusiasm. "Why the silence on the trip?"

Christina stopped. "Let's just say I've had a lot of things to think about. I debated whether I would bring it up." She held out her hand so Miki could pull her up. "You thought I was upset because you're . . ."

Miki easily pulled her up. They were inches from each other. "Wouldn't be the first time."

"I'm sorry." Christina touched Miki's arm. "I am sorry," she said very softly. Her eyes were unguardedly honest. "I can imagine what you must have been thinking."

Miki stepped away from her touch. Wondering if she knew how God blessed desirable she was. She collected the discarded sandwich wrappers and emptied the last of her coffee on the ground. The warm liquid melted the snow and made a tiny dark brown crater.

"What's wrong?" Christina asked, sensing Miki's shift in mood.

"This is getting messy." Miki clenched her hands into fists. This was a rare emotion, she thought. She seldom allowed anger to control her. Anger or desire? Miki felt as if all her emotions had been dumped into a cup and an unseen hand was shaking them up and down.

"What?"

"The investigation, Christina. That's why I'm here." Her voice took on an assertive tone. Good, she thought, she needed to be more assertive.

Christina held up her hands, a puzzled frown on her face "Maybe I'm missing something here, but how does this . . ."

Miki drew in a deep ragged breath. "Look, why don't we go

back." She knelt down and snapped the clasps on her backpack. She rubbed her fingers against her lips as she thought about her next words. "I'm not upset with you. I just need to step back from this a minute. Think about some things."

"I don't understand."

"This is the first time my sexuality has been dragged into the middle of an investigation." As the excuse limped out of her mouth, Miki realized that her words lacked conviction.

"But it doesn't matter to me. I told you—"

"Christina," Miki cut her off. A mindless frustration enveloped her. "Let me just think about this, okay?"

Miki read the confusion in her eyes, but all Christina did was nod.

The ride back was uninterrupted. Miki did not stop to inquire if Christina was cold. The roar of the snowmobile engine served to protect the silence. She stopped in front of Christina's house.

Christina swung her leg off the seat. "Could we talk about this?"

"Soon." Miki said as she revved up the engine and pulled back onto the road.

In her cabin, Miki replayed her conversation with Christina and knew that she had been less than honest. Somewhere between Christmas and now she had smashed headlong into love and didn't know what the hell to do about it. If Christina had been gay, they'd have been in bed already, but she wasn't and Miki knew she could not go there. An affair with Christina, even if she wanted it, would mean a long-term commitment. Miki opened the wood stove and tossed another log on. She watched as the fire licked up the side of the white birch bark; the flames turning red, then blue and finally yellow. A long-term commitment meant she'd never advance beyond the rank of sergeant. There were gay cops in relationships, Miki thought, but they were truly the silent majority in Maine.

Chapter Fifteen

Miki stopped at the sheriff's office around noon the next day. Martin Luther King Day, Miki thought. The only people off were nonessential federal, state and county employees. Emergency personnel had to work, regardless. She could see Scott talking to Janey, their backs to the door. She had called Christina's house four times before she left for the sheriff's office, but there was no answer.

She stepped inside, unprepared for the visceral response she had when she was face to face with Scott. She glared at him.

He licked his lips and smiled. "Understand from Janey that Christina has gone back to Boston."

Miki looked from Scott to Janey.

"She called early this morning. Said some unexpected business came up and she would be gone for several days." Janey sighed, clearly unaware of the tension between Miki and Scott. "Maybe it's for the best. She's been through a lot."

"Probably went back to her husband." Scott's full lips twisted into an obscene sneer.

Miki gripped the door handle. She wished it was Scott's neck.

"You're right. It's for the best," Miki said to Janey, dismissing Scott with her body language. "Has an arraignment date been set for Billy Clark yet?"

"Since he's out on bail, the judge set the arraignment for next week."

"Has he gotten a lawyer yet?"

"Yeah." Janey sat down at her desk. "Interesting. He got Bob Carter. He's the best in the county when it comes to criminal law and also the most expensive. I didn't expect him to have that kind of money."

"No I wouldn't have expected it either. Peter around?" Miki asked. Miki noted Scott's silence.

"He's in his office."

Miki brushed past Scott. She found him easy to ignore. She stepped into Peter's office.

"You want Scott in here?"

"No. I just wanted to talk with you, Peter." Miki eased herself down into the chair across from his desk.

"You've done good work. Caught Billy Clark and worked out an agreement with the woman over access. The county commissioners have agreed to call a meeting of the Bass Fishermen's Association. It's scheduled for tomorrow, I'd like you there."

"Whoa, you're going too fast. What agreement?"

"Oh, I thought Mrs. Reynolds told you. She called me last night and said she wanted all the problems behind her. She said she'd agree to pay for a survey of the south line of her property so the town could put a road in. She probably wanted to surprise you. Told me to tell the commissioners and anyone else that had to be notified. I told her I would."

Miki was silent.

"She gave you the credit. Said you had proposed the idea, and after she'd thought about it, she liked it. She asked me to get a surveyor in. You done good, Mik. Caught the bad guy, resolved the land issue. You should be pleased. I expect now you'll be getting back to Jackman."

Miki rubbed her chin. "Yes," she said, still not focusing on Peter's words. "Janey told me Clark hired Bobby Carter as his lawyer. I've checked on his background, and he doesn't have that kind of money. Guy lives in a shack up at Greely Point, a shack he doesn't even own."

"Look, Mik, he could be one of those trust fund hippies or one of those city escapees who dumped a big job and moved to the sticks. There could be tons of money buried in Pamper boxes in the backyard."

"Maybe."

"So what are your plans?"

Miki looked up. "Plans?"

"About going back to Jackman. You'll have to come back for the trial, but other than that I don't think you're needed here."

"I haven't thought that far ahead." Miki stood up. "I'll let you know my plans later, Peter."

"I want you at that Bass Association meeting tomorrow." Miki knew his tone suggested no compromise.

"I'll be there." Miki closed the door behind her. Scott was gone, and Janey was alone in the office. She looked up expectantly. "Did Mrs. Reynolds say anything else?" Miki asked.

"I think she wanted to, but she didn't. Hey, I've seen that frown before. What's wrong?"

Miki shook her head. "I don't know, there's just something bothering me about this case."

"Well, Scott sure seems happy?"

"Happy, how?"

"I don't know. Hard to explain. Like he thinks he's won something. He's such a snake. I prefer it when he's in his dark and gloomy moods. When he's happy, I worry."

⊷⊶

Miki left the sheriff's office and turned her truck toward Greely Point. She was uncertain what she was going to say or do, but she had to talk with Billy Clark. She could see smoke curling from his roof. The weathered cedar shingles on the outside of the cabin looked as though they had lost their battle with Mother Nature. The roof sagged, and there were newspaper and rags stuffed into the broken windows. She unsnapped the clasp that held her gun in the holster and eased herself out of the truck. Clark's face suddenly appeared in the smeared window. "What ya want?" The window muffled his voice.

"To talk to you." She stayed by her truck. There was a long delay. She wondered what she would do if he came out shooting.

Finally, the door cracked open. Billy Clark peeked around, and she realized he was looking for her gun. She kept her right hand on her truck door and her left hand at her side.

He stepped outside but kept the door open to his back so he could make a hasty retreat. "What ya want," he said again.

"To talk." Miki didn't move.

"So talk."

"Can I come closer?"

Billy Clark studied her.

She stepped away from the truck. "How about a cup of coffee."

"I ain't in a mood to socialize."

"We might be able to help each other."

"How?"

Miki motioned toward the house. "Let's talk inside." She walked carefully toward him, stopping when she reached the steps.

Billy moved aside, and she went past him into the cabin. There was an unmade bed in the corner. A large 27-inch color television was in the other corner with a brand-new easy chair nearby. Miki had noticed the small satellite dish on the front lawn. A stove, small refrigerator, sink and kitchen table were on the other side. There was a door, which probably led to a bathroom.

"Got any coffee?"

Billy kept his distance from her. "Yeah." A Mr. Coffee machine sat on the small counter near the sink. He reached for a cup in the open cupboard, looked inside, dumped whatever had been living in the cup on the counter, wiped it with his hand and poured the coffee. He stepped back across the room, extended his arm as far as it would go and handed the mug to Miki.

"Thanks." She sipped at the coffee and willed herself not to react. It tasted greasy.

"What you want." He remained suspicious.

Miki took another sip of the coffee. This was real acting, she decided as she swallowed. "Wanted to talk with you."

"So talk."

She set the cup on the kitchen table and nodded to a chair. "Mind if I sit down?" When he didn't acknowledge her question, she pulled out a chair and sat down, careful to keep nothing between her and Billy. "I checked your record."

He scowled.

"You lived in a lot of places. Been in a lot of places."

"That's behind me."

"I see you spent time at the City Mental Health Center, just last year."

"That's not in my arrest record."

"It gets there when you tell a judge you can't show up for court because you checked yourself in there."

"So?"

"So what you check yourself in for, Billy?"

"That ain't none of your business."

He was right, but she said, "It is my business Billy. You made it my business when you tried to break into Mrs. Reynold's house, and when you took a crowbar to the side of my face." She gestured to her stitches.

"What you want?"

"Just to talk to you, Billy."

"I got a lawyer. I don't need to talk to you." Triumph gleamed in his eyes.

"No, you don't. This is just a friendly visit." Miki leaned forward, and Billy jumped. He licked nervously at his lips. "You know, you tell me who put you up to this and you won't see any jail time."

"I ain't going to see any jail time. Anyway, my attorney said a plea bargain's going to get me off."

"The assistant district attorney is a friend of mine. No plea bargain. She says she's going to ask for maximum sentence, and that means jail time. A judge maybe won't go high, but he'll make it high enough that you're going to spend some time behind bars."

Billy shifted from one foot to the other, and Miki watched his eyes. "I'll get me a jury. Won't buy anything you say."

Miki leaned forward again, knowing her size was imposing. "Think of all those women on the jury. Think about how the district attorney is going to remind them that it could have been their house, their window you tried to climb through."

Billy wiped his mouth. "You can't prove nothin'."

"I can prove you were trying to break into her house. I can prove you had a crowbar with you. I can prove, Billy"—Miki stood up and took a step toward him— "that you had more on your mind than just scaring her."

"You ain't got nothin'. My friend said—"

"Friend? What friend, Billy?"

"You get out of here. I'm going to call my lawyer." Miki eyed him. She had seen the caged-animal syndrome before. Billy was sweating, uncertain where to look. He couldn't look at Miki but clearly didn't want to keep staring at the floor.

Miki wanted to shake him, yank him off his feet and hold him high over her head. Instead, she smiled at him calmly. "Think about it. You tell your friend that I know someone put you up to this," she said as she stepped closer to him. "You tell your friend I'm going to find out who he is, and then I'm coming after him. You tell your friend all of that." Miki snapped her fingers, and Billy jumped. "Then, when I'm done with your friend, I'm coming after you."

Miki headed to the door. "Tell him, Billy," she ordered. She made a lot of noise getting into her truck and driving off. She suspected that the telephone lines to Jackman would be burning up once he called his attorney and the attorney called the colonel. But Miki knew she had gotten a response and that Billy was going to do something. She drove about three miles down the road and parked her truck deep in the trees where she had left her snowmobile, then took the snowmobile back toward Billy Clark's property. She parked a distance away from the house so he wouldn't hear the snowmobile.

She didn't have to wait long. Clark's ancient truck came out of his driveway and turned right toward town. Miki let him get a ways down the road before she ran to her snowmobile and followed. He drove past the spot where she had hidden her truck. He was apparently too focused on the road to notice it. At an abandoned gasoline and convenience store, she parked her snowmobile a distance away and followed him on foot. He looked for something in his jacket pocket, then got out of his car and walked to the pay phone.

He fumbled in his pants pocket for change, peered at the paper in his hand and punched in a number. Miki could see him talking, but she was too far away to hear. His frustration when he hung up the phone, however, showed. He reached in his pocket again and pulled out another piece of paper. He punched in a second number.

Again she saw his mouth moving, and again he slammed down the receiver.

Miki waited until he left, then walked to the telephone. She wrote down the number. She knew she didn't have to follow Billy; he was going back to his cabin. Miki stayed off the road and headed to her truck, where she loaded up her snowmobile, switched on the truck's ignition to power up her cellular telephone.

She called Augusta and talked to one of the officers there. She could expect a list of the calls made from that telephone the next day. Miki was pleased. All in all, she thought, she was making progress. Now all she had to do was figure out what she was going to tell the members of the Bass Association. That meeting was scheduled for early in the morning.

Chapter Sixteen

Miki had agreed to meet Peter at the county courthouse at eight a.m. When she arrived, the parking lot was full. She prayed it was a heavy court day and that most people were hoping for justice and not an explanation on local access and fishing. She ran an anxious hand through her hair.

"Great turnout," Peter enthused as he opened the door for her. "I expect all the publicity about the arrest has brought out the curious as well as the bass fishermen. I told the commissioners we'd give a statement, then open it to questions. Since it's an election year, I thought I'd make the opening statement." Peter chuckled at his own joke. "You can answer the questions."

"What do you want me to say?"

"Just outline her proposal. What we talked about on the telephone this morning. Pretty cut and dried." They turned right into the hallway that led to the commission chambers.

"How much convincing do you think we'll have to do?

"Don't know." Peter opened the door. "But I'm sure we're going to find out."

Miki stopped when she saw all of the people, Kristan had a front row seat. Miki stood next to Peter. Kristan winked at her friend just as Commissioner Jason Saddlon rapped the meeting to order. The buzz stopped. Miki put a hand to her throat, certain her tongue was glued to the top of her mouth. Visions of her high school speech class raced through her mind; there were no fond memories. She focused on what Peter was telling the group. "Course we have the Ranger here to thank," he said by way of closing. "Questions?"

"How do we know she'll keep her word?" Keith Shipman asked.

Peter turned to Miki. "In addition to giving her word—" Miki said.

"Can't hear you," someone shouted from the back of the room.

"In addition to giving her word," Miki raised her voice, "Mrs. Reynolds has agreed to sign a ninety-nine year lease with the county. In exchange for donating land for a public road, the county has agreed to put it in and maintain it." There were more questions about legal liability and public access.

"How she doing?" a woman asked.

Peter answered. "Just fine. Mrs. Reynolds has been through a lot. She is in Boston right now, but we expect her back anytime."

"What's going to happen to Billy Clark?" Keith asked.

"Now, Keith, you know that's an ongoing investigation and we can't talk about it," the sheriff chided.

Jason rapped his gavel. "Any more questions about land access or rights?" He looked around the room expectantly. "Well, then, thank you, Peter, and you, too, Ranger. I declare this meeting adjourned."

"Great job," Kristan whispered to Miki.

"I am out of here."

On Tuesday evening, Miki was back in her cabin, her feet propped up on the table she had turned into a desk. She was studying the log the phone company had sent her. She was interested in two calls, one to Billy's lawyer and the other to the sheriff's department.

Billy's attorney had called the colonel. He was irate and charged that Miki had violated Billy's right to have his lawyer present when he was questioned. When the colonel called Miki earlier that afternoon, she told him that she had not meant to violate Billy's rights but had simply been overzealous. She had agreed she would not go near him again, and that was when he had stopped yelling at her.

The other call, Miki knew, was to Scott. Although Janey said the caller had not identified himself, she said a man had tried to reach Scott on Monday afternoon. When she told him Scott wasn't in, he hung up on her. Janey confirmed that it was not the first time that man had called and asked for Scott.

Although it didn't prove anything, it did confirm something Miki had suspected. Scott was either mucking around in her case, or he was somehow involved in it. But if he was, she couldn't figure out why.

The telephone interrupted her thoughts. She looked at the clock; it was ten p.m. Miki decided to let the answering machine take it. She heard a click and then Christina's voice apologizing for calling so late. Miki almost tumbled out of her chair as she scrambled to answer the telephone. "Don't hang up."

"Miki?"

"Where are you? When did you get back?"

"At home. I got back just a little while ago"

Miki hesitated. "Are you all right?"

"Yes." Christina answered softly. "I know it's late, but I'd like to talk. I don't want to wait until tomorrow. Could you come over?"

Miki agreed, and they hung up. She threw on her black running pants with white stripes running down the legs and a black and red shirt. Twenty minutes later she was there.

"Come in," Christina motioned to the living room.

Miki followed her and stood near one of the chairs.

"This seems very difficult," Christina said. Miki sensed her agitation. "But I don't want it to be. Really. Please sit down. A drink? Coffee?"

Miki chose a chair away from the sofa where Christina had been sitting. "Coffee, thanks." Miki willed herself not to fidget.

Christina returned from the kitchen with a large mug of coffee and handed it to her. "I'm not going to bite." Her laugh helped to resolve some of the tension. Miki smiled. "I owe you an apology for leaving." Christina sat down on the sofa. "I should have called you and told you, but I didn't—" She looked down at her hands, which were clenched together. She unclasped them and spread her fingers wide. Then she put her hands on her lap.

"Do you want to talk about it?"

Christina smiled. "I had this speech all prepared, but it's not going to work. Let's just say I need to think about some things, and I had to come back here to do it."

Miki sipped at her coffee. She had a thousand questions, and for the first time since they had met, she felt unsettled. "Are you all right?"

"Yes," Christina said obliquely. "I had a good trip. I talked about you with my ex-husband."

Miki was in mid-sip when she heard that. The coffee caught in her throat, and she began to cough. She put both hands over her mouth. She felt as if her throat had closed and she was going to choke. Christina raced over, a napkin in her hand. The blood rushed to Miki's face. Tears were streaming from her eyes. She found it difficult to breath. She raised her arms over her head, just as Christina handed her the napkin. Air rushed into her lungs. "I'm okay." she croaked feeling like an idiot.

"Would you like some water?"

"No." Miki coughed, her arms still up.

"Should I pat you on the back?"

Miki shook her head. "I'm okay. What exactly did you tell your husband?" she said between coughs. She wiped the tears from her eyes and rubbed the napkin against her nose. She had the impulse to flee but willed herself back in her chair.

"Everything."

"What exactly does that mean?" Miki coughed again.

Christina frowned. "Oh, I understand." Christina laughed. "I'm sorry. I talk over everything with John—we're best of friends, I told you that."

"How did he react?"

"Like John. Pragmatic. You have to know him."

Again no more explanation and more silence. "What's going on?"

Christina looked down at her open palms. "I thought this would be so easy, but it's not. I just need time to sort some things out. It has to do with me, not you," she said.

Miki walked to the window and looked out at the moon. She was a trained interviewer, but Christina clearly needed space. Now who's avoiding, she thought. "Peter's happy. We met with the county commissioners and members of the Bass Association this morning, and it looks like they've agreed to your easement idea."

"That's great." Christina was clearly pleased. "But it was your easement idea, remember?"

"Well, it doesn't matter." Miki turned and looked at Christina.

Christina added several logs to the fire. She gestured at the wood. "I ordered this, and I did some of my own splitting." She brushed the bark off her hands. "Anything about Clark?"

"He'll be arraigned next week. Then he can either plead or ask for a trial."

Miki didn't tell Christina about her confrontation with Clark.

"What do you think will happen?"

"I don't know. The holiday delayed things, I have an appointment to talk to Jennifer the first of the week. He can try for a plea bargain, but I don't think Jennifer will go along with it."

"Good."

"But if he decides to go to trial? Well, it's risky."

"Risky?"

"He could convince a jury that he was just walking to the lake, but I doubt any sane jury would buy it. And . . ." Miki paused. "You'd have to testify."

Christina looked away. "I hadn't thought about that. There's no other way?"

"No." Miki had not moved from the window.

Christina stared openly at her. "I'm sorry I left."

Miki waited for her to say more. "I'm glad you're back."

"Me too."

Miki gazed into Christina's eyes. She stifled the urge to go to her and take her in her arms. The tension was riveting, but little more was said before Miki left.

Miki spent the rest of the week focused on the investigation. She did a quiet background check on Scott and found nothing. She was certain Scott was involved, but she lacked proof. She stayed away from Billy Clark; she was not prepared to lose her job over this, but from a distance she watched him unravel. A chance meeting at the gasoline station sent him running out the door.

Miki ignored messages from Kristan, but not the last one, because Kristan had threatened to hunt her down.

As Miki parked her truck in front of Kristan's office, Kristan was coming out of the sheriff's office. "That's it, you're not going to get away."

"I know, I know. I'm here to see you."

"Good," She tugged Miki along by her arm. "I'm pissed at you. I've called and left messages. I know you've been around because I've seen your truck in town." Kristan pushed her office door open. "I'm not going to let you go until you tell me what the hell is going on." Although Kristan was a lot smaller, Miki knew better then to resist when Kristan was this annoyed. Kristan slammed the door closed, then knocked her telephone off the hook. "What's going on?"

Mik studied her fingertips.

"Am I supposed to guess?" Kristan's anger was mounting.

"No."

"So tell me?"

"Okay," Miki said to halt the onslaught of questions.

Kristan leaned back in her desk chair and put her feet on the desk. "In this lifetime or the next?"

"You don't have to be such a jerk, even if you are my best friend."

"Miki, I have a news story to write here . . ."

"You know that Christina is back from Boston."

"I heard. Why did she leave."

"I'm not sure, but before she left we talked about my being gay."

"Was she upset?"

"No. She said Scott had told her just days before. I don't think she cared one way or the other. The day after we had dinner at your place she wanted to talk about it."

"Am I missing something here? If she's not upset, then what's going on?"

"That's what I can't figure out, and she won't tell me."

Kristan rocked in her chair. "How's she acting?"

"Quiet. We've not been together much, and when we are we talk about everything, except what's bothering her."

"Maybe she's trying to sort through how she feels about you."

"You mean as in . . ." Miki groped for a response, then realized what Kristan meant. "No, no. Remember, she's straight. She was married."

"So? That's not a lifetime condition. Women who start out straight can end up with women. Are you worried she might be confusing her need for you as a cop with who you are as a woman?"

"Probably yes. Hell, I can't explain it."

"Has she said anything at all to indicate"—Kristan's hand make a little seesaw gesture—"to indicate that she might . . . you know."

"I don't know!" Miki snapped, utterly exasperated. "This is so stupid."

"Miki, I don't know what to tell you. I've never experienced anything like this before, but maybe this will help. One of the reasons I have been trying so hard to get hold of you is that Jennifer and I are having our annual cabin fever party tomorrow. I know it isn't much time, but why don't you invite her? There will be a mix of people straight and gay, and you can see how she reacts."

Miki frowned. "Straights."

"Of course, Mik. There aren't enough gay people to go around in Bailey's Cove. Two reporter friends of mine and Toby and his new girlfriend are invited. There'll be folks from the courthouse, people who work with Jennifer. Jackie said she can make it, and she's invited people from the clinic. Angela and Theresa—you had dinner with them last year—who own the motel. Three or four other lesbian couples that I've met who live over in Bayport said they would come, and these two gay guys who run a B&B. You know almost everyone."

Miki hesitated. She'd heard about their party, but had never been able to come down from Jackman for it.

"You don't have to do anything but stand around and watch. It'll be a wicked good time. Let's see how she reacts to the mix of people. Who knows, she might even hate it," Kristan said teasingly.

"That's what I'm afraid of."

"And then again she might love it," Kristan added.

"I don't know. The get-together at your house went well, but this is a party. I don't do well at parties even without all this pressure." Miki scratched her forehead. "What if she's turned off by it? Won't there be women dancing with women, men dancing with men. What if she walks out? I don't think I could handle that."

"And there'll be women dancing with men. Look, I've spent only an evening with Christina, but I can tell you this, you've got to cut her some slack. Miki, you're hedging this. You can't hide your friendship with her under some kind of rock."

"I'll ask. But I'm going to warn her about the mix of people."

"I wouldn't want it any other way."

Chapter Seventeen

Miki stood in the shower thinking about Christina. When she had called to tell her about the party, she had eagerly accepted, but when Miki offered to pick her up, she had demurred saying she would prefer to drive in case Miki wanted to stay longer. Something in Christina's voice suggested there was no room for discussion.

She glanced at the clock. They had agreed to meet at Kristan's at eight, She hastily toweled down and stared at her closet. Her choices were few. Most of her clothes were summer wear. She selected a black pair of pants and white shirt and her blue leather jacket.

Miki was determined not to keep Christina waiting. Butterflies kept dancing in her chest, and she was there in minutes. Christina's Mercedes was already parked in the driveway.

"Hi," Miki said as she opened the door. Christina's cologne wafted from inside the car. Miki held on to the side of the car with her other hand, fearful that her knees would buckle.

"I'm looking forward to my first party in Bailey's Cove." Christina looked up at her.

"Me, too."

Kristan opened the door on the first knock. "Hey, buddy, come in, come in."

Jennifer gave Miki a big hug, but Miki stiffened, afraid of Christina's reaction.

"Christina, I'm so glad you could join us," Jennifer said as she hugged her too.

"Thank you. I had a great time the last time I was here."

"I brought you some stuff, beer, wine . . ." Suddenly feeling shy, Miki handed Jennifer her packages.

"Thank you." She slipped her arm through Miki's and pulled her into the kitchen. "Let me take your coat. Kristan," she called over her shoulder, "why don't you take Christina's coat and introduce her to everybody. Miki can help me in here."

As directed, Miki poured potato chips into a bowl, then reached into the refrigerator and put a bowl of dip on the counter. "Is everything all right?"

Miki looked at Jennifer intently, searching for words that would help Jennifer see Christina through her eyes. "I know Kristan told you what's going on. She said she tells you everything." Miki paused. "Christina reminds me of you."

"Me?"

"Yeah, you're pretty and"—Miki hesitated as she chose her words— "you both have that quality that makes people feel comfortable around you. I suspect that's what Kristan saw in you."

"Thank you, Miki." Jennifer smiled. "That's nice of you to say, but I'm not in Christina's league. She's a classic beauty, like something out of a painting. That hair, those eyes. This is such a cliché, but when she walks into a room, you turn to look. She is that beautiful. But I suspect one of the reasons she likes you is that you see beyond the surface, and that, my friend, makes you very special." She hugged Miki. "Come on, the music's started again. Let's go rescue our respective partners."

Miki followed Jennifer into the living and dining rooms where clusters of people stood. She searched for Christina and saw her talking with Jackie. Christina turned to look at Miki at the same moment.

Jennifer noticed the look that passed between them and said, "Why don't you go visit with Christina and Jackie? I have to find Kristan."

Miki made her way across the room, stopping to talk with people who greeted her. Jackie spotted Miki and gave a hoot. Her arms out, she wrapped her in a bear hug. Warm and infectious, Jackie's exuberance washed over her. She held Miki at arms length. "Glad you came tonight."

"Me, too." Miki smiled.

"I was just telling Christina"—Jackie turned to her—"that I would love to have her visit the clinic. She said she worked in one while she was still in school."

"I was just a receptionist, answered the telephone, hardly enough to qualify as someone important at a clinic," Christina stammered.

Jackie laughed. "You should talk with my receptionist. She'll tell you she's the first line of defense." Jackie held up her hand. "Don't get me started. I love the woman, but you would think that clinic wouldn't operate if she wasn't there."

"Well, I'd like to see it." She turned to Miki, "I told Kristan I'd like to see her office also." They glanced over to where Kristan was talking with Jennifer.

Jackie looked up when she heard her name from across the room. "Excuse me just a moment. That's my nurse over there who demands my attention." Jackie went over and hugged a rather portly woman and her male companion.

"I really like your friends," Christina said.

"I'm glad." Miki pushed her hands into her pockets and stared down at her feet. "Can I get you something to drink?"

"In a minute. I think first you have to tell me what you're so worried about."

"Well, I guess I'm not sure how you're going to react to all these people." Miki stopped, the warmth of her embarrassment creeping up her cheeks.

"Ah." A teasing smile played on Christina's mouth. "I'm glad you invited me."

They helped themselves to some food and then mingled with the others. The music was slow and easy, and they watched as couples danced. Jennifer had just joined them when suddenly the deejay yelled, "Hey everybody, our hostess has requested a rocker, and she wants everyone to dance."

"Do you dance, Christina?" Jennifer asked as Chubby Checker's "Twist" began to play. Miki inwardly groaned. She didn't like to dance.

Christina said with a laugh. "We do dance in Boston."

"Great," Jennifer said. "Any problems dancing with a woman? My friend Miki here is a great dancer." She nudged Miki toward the dining room, where everyone already was dancing.

"I think I'm up to the challenge." Christina looked sideways at Miki.

Miki wanted to collapse. She wondered if she could feign a heart attack. A stroke would be nice right now, she thought. When she realized she couldn't leave Christina standing alone at the edge of the dance floor, she reluctantly followed her. She felt as if Jennifer had asked her to step in front of a firing squad. She was all arms and legs, and she could feel the perspiration trickle down her back. Christina by contrast seemed cool and relaxed.

As the last few beats of the song played out, Miki could hear others laughing and talking around her. She had been so focused on Christina that she had stopped hearing anything but the music.

"That was nice." Christina stopped in the middle of the floor, fanning her face with her hand. "I haven't danced in years."

"It was fun." Miki looked around as she heard the first few beats of Michael Bolton's "A Love So Beautiful." Miki swallowed, trying to think of a graceful way for them to exit the floor. Miki held out her hand. "Would you like to?"

"Dance? Yes." Christina stepped close to Miki. "It would be easier if you put your arms around me." She looked teasingly into Miki's eyes.

Miki raised her arms and felt Christina slide into them. She was unsure of how or where her feet were going, but they seemed to move.

She held her close. Christina's perfume was intoxicating. She could smell it in her hair and on her clothes. A buzz surged through her brain as her sensory nerves booted up and then crashed.

She closed her eyes. She remembered the time she had found an abandoned fawn in the woods. She had picked it up gently, its body warm against hers. She had rubbed her chin against the fawn's head to try and send a message to it that it was safe. The fawn raised its head, and Miki remembered how it felt when its soft mouth nuzzled her chin.

Miki touched her cheek against Christina's hair. She wanted to bury her face in her hair, kiss her eyes. Christina moved closer, and Miki felt Christina melting against her. The touch was so sensuous, so pleasing, that Miki felt every nerve of her body tingle.

Sweat trickled down her back. The hand that held Christina's felt sticky. She wanted to stop and wipe it on her pants. Christina let go of Miki's hand and put both her arms around Miki's neck. Miki rested both her hands on Christina's waist and resisted the urge to pull her tighter against her. She willed the music to keep playing.

As they swayed to the music, Christina's nose was close to Miki's throat, and she could feel the warm breath on her skin. It felt like a gentle caress.

Miki moved her hand farther up Christina's back, and Christina's hand moved down and rested low on Miki's hip. Christina's breasts pressed against her body. Somehow their feet had stopped, and only their hips were moving.

Oh, Michael, keep singing, Miki silently prayed.

When the music stopped, Miki reluctantly dropped her arms

and stepped back. Christina's eyes were distant, unfocused, and when she finally looked at Miki, they seemed to slice through Miki's heart.

"I've got to go." Christina's voice was hoarse.

Miki nodded.

"Would you make my excuses?"

"I want to go with you," Miki said, her mind a blur of hope and desire.

"I want—" Christina stopped. She placed a hand on Miki's arm. "We'll talk later."

Miki opened her mouth, but words refused to jump from her brain to her mouth. She watched Christina push through the crowd still on the dance floor. Friends stood laughing, talking, waiting for the next song to begin. Miki felt a weariness creep over her. The shadow coming towards her was Kristan. "Mik, you okay?"

"I'm in love, and I don't know what to do about it." Tears stung her eyes as she turned away.

Miki lay on her couch. She watched the flames from the wood stove dance on her ceiling. Her mood sunk deeper. She had left the party shortly after Christina, giving her time to get out of the driveway and away before she went out.

Jennifer had apologized, upset that encouraging them to dance had caused Christina to leave. But Miki knew Christina had felt the same breathless rush, the lingering want that she had felt.

Miki inhaled. No more running away. She got up, threw on her jacket and hastily pulled shoes over her bare feet. Outside her feet sank and were awash in snow and ice.

She climbed into her truck and drove toward Christina's house. No more games, no more golden webs of uncertainty. She had to know exactly how Christina felt and why she had left.

The lights in the house were on upstairs and down. Miki had raised her fist to knock when the door opened. Christina stood there, in white silk lounging pajamas, backlit by the living room lamps. Her black hair glistened. Miki could barely swallow. She stepped inside and closed the door behind her. She threw her jacket on the floor. Christina's eyes told her everything.

"Don't talk." Christina said as she reached out and touched Miki's lips. Miki almost expected electricity to arc between them.

Miki gently placed her hands on Christina's shoulders. The silk that covered them was exotic, the warmth and softness of her body was intoxicating. She kissed her hair, then pulled back. Christina's eyes were feverish, her lips swollen. Miki's desire exploded with no interlude and no moment of exploration. She kissed her hard.

Miki heard the low growl as Christina responded. Their tongues hungry and eager, Miki pulled Christina's hips into hers, and Christina gasped.

Then Christina's mouth was on hers with a yearning that astounded her. Her hands slid up to Miki's cheeks, and she pulled Miki's mouth even closer. Miki felt an insatiable thirst, a craving that at first flamed and then detonated within her. She kissed Christina's eyes, her cheeks, her neck. She slid her hands under Christina's shirt and savored the raw heat she felt against her fingertips.

They kissed again, their tongues seeking each other's sweetness, exploring, pushing the boundaries of boldness. Breathless, she picked Christina up and carried her to the sofa. Christina kissed Miki's ear, and her tongue lingered inside. Miki felt a shiver race through her body.

Fingers numb with desire fumbled with the buttons on her pajamas. Frustrated that her hands would not respond to so simple a task, Miki pulled the shirt apart and the buttons flew like tiny rockets into the air. She was momentarily startled by the beauty of Christina's breasts, the nipples dark and inviting. Her tongue caressed first one and then the other.

Christina gasped then pulled Miki to her. "I want to feel you all over," Christina whispered against Miki's hair.

Miki ripped off her shirt and pants, then slipped the silk pajama bottoms down over Christina's smooth white hips, savoring each curve, each fold, and those inviting thighs.

Miki lay across her, their breasts touching, their hips together, their lips on a search-and-rescue mission of pleasure. Christina pulled Miki even tighter against her as Miki traced her tongue down Christina's neck, kissing each shoulder and down her arms, her tongue trailing over her wrists, sucking the tips of each finger.

Christina's nipples puckered like spring buds on a young maple tree. Miki's hands caressed them as her tongue explored, pulling even more sweetness from Christina's body.

Christina's breathing was ragged. Her chest heaved. Desire exploding between her thighs, she begged Miki not to stop. "Oh God, kiss me again," she said between clenched teeth. Christina's groaning was almost a sob as she pulled her tighter as if her passion were awakening for the first time, Miki thought.

She moved down and drew a trail with her tongue around Christina's nipples, tasting the sweet salt of her skin. Her mouth moved lower and licked at the curls of hair below, which tickled her tongue. Miki's hand touched the hot fountain between Christina's thighs, and Christina bucked.

Miki's tongue followed where her hand had led, her tongue burying deep inside Christina's folds, bathing in her wetness. She felt Christina shiver and push her hips against her. Groaning, Christina dug her fingers into Miki's wrists.

Christina clenched as an orgasm shook her, then she lay back panting. Miki kissed her belly.

"I'll never get enough of you." Miki saw the tears, before she heard the sob. "Oh God, I've made you cry."

She held Christina against her, the tears hot against her throat. She kissed the top of her head then licked the tears from her eyes.

"I've never felt like that before." Christina stopped. "I want you again," she said against Miki's lips. Miki's arms tightened around Christina. She wanted to go slow, but Christina's urgency and Miki's need erupted, and together they climbed the mountain of ecstasy.

Miki lay next to Christina in her king-size bed, Christina's head on her shoulder, her black hair a soft blanket on her arm and neck. They had made love all night. At first Christina was shy as she explored Miki's body, but as she understood the pleasure she was giving, she became bold, ardent, even aggressive.

"You're awake."

"Um." Miki kissed the top of her head.

"I can't believe I fell asleep."

"We both fell asleep."

"What time is it?"

Miki looked over at the clock on the dresser. "Ten."

Christina asked shyly. "What do we do now?"

"What would you like to do?"

Christina propped herself up and looked at Miki.

"I think I know." Miki kissed her eyes, her mouth. She pulled Christina on top of her and let her tongue trace a line down the side of her neck. She felt Christina shiver.

The night before they had chased passion at warp speed, but this morning their lovemaking was languid and lazy. Miki touched and stroked every part of Christina's body. She loved the low growl Christina made just before she climaxed.

Afterwards, Miki savored the sensation of Christina's warm body spooned in front of her. "You remember when I came back from Boston, and I told you I had things to think about?"

Miki raised up on her elbow. "Yes."

"This was it."

"Making love?"

Christina rolled onto her back and looked at Miki. "I don't think I had quite taken it to that level, but I realized I felt something different. I found myself thinking about you all the time, especially after that day we split wood together. I realized I'd been staring at your body, the muscles in your arms, the way your breasts strained against your shirt, but I didn't know what to do with it." She traced a finger down Miki's arm. "I was confused and overwhelmed. I don't ever remember looking at a woman quite that way before, appreciating the angles, the lines." Christina's finger touched Miki's mouth and traced the angle of her lips. "I thought it all somehow had gotten mixed up with my dependency. You know the strong woman who carries a gun protecting a weaker woman. It was something I'd never ever experienced before. Then last night when we danced," Christina sighed. "Well, let's just say I don't know what I would have done if you hadn't come over last night."

Miki kissed each of Christina's fingers and smiled. "I never realized splitting wood could be so sensuous. I still marvel that I didn't put the maul through my shin. I was watching the way you bent over, how you lifted each piece of wood and threw it on the pile. The way those lavender pants stretched across your hips. That silk blouse." Miki swallowed. "I found myself watching you every moment. Even in church on Christmas Eve when I should have been listening to the sermon."

"When Janey sang the *Ave Maria* I cried." Christina's dark eyes looked deeply into Miki's. "I felt silly, but it was so hauntingly beautiful and I felt so alone. Lonely in a crowded church. I missed my dad, my mom. All the people I ever loved. And I couldn't figure out what I was doing in a small church in Maine and . . ." Christina pushed hair off of Miki's forehead. "I like the way you hair falls down on your forehead. It touches your eyebrows." She kissed her gently. "How about breakfast?"

"How about a shower, together," Miki offered.

"I've never taken a shower with anyone else. What do we do?"

"More of the same, only in water." Miki grinned impishly.

"You're a heel," Miki said to herself for the hundredth time. Monday morning, Miki found herself in her truck on the way to Jackman. She had gone to her cabin with Christina on Sunday afternoon to get a change of clothes, and her message machine told her the colonel wanted to see her Monday.

The message was brief with no explanation of why and no invitation to call him at home Sunday. She ignored three messages from Kristan. She saw the confusion in Christina's eyes when she hadn't asked her to go along. She also saw the insecurity when Miki was evasive about when she would return.

Miki needed time to think, and being near Christina left her distracted. Christina would want a future together, she was sure. Things had moved forward at such a wild pleasure-mad speed that Miki felt like she was on Rollerblades on a San Francisco hill. Everything was out of control. She could hear Kristan now: "You're a jerk, Miki Jamieson. The woman of your dreams falls in love with you, and you go running to Jackman."

She was running all right, Miki thought, speeding to Jackman, but uncertain if she was running away or toward something.

Two hours later, Miki felt mentally drained as she stood before the colonel. "Sit, sit, you did a good job down there. I've spoken several times with Peter. Everything I sent you to do you accomplished. I understand the parties have all agreed to a right-of-way, and Peter says the trouble is over. I'm pleased, Miki."

"Thank you, sir."

"Now I have another problem. There have been a rash of camp breaks—" He shuffled through some papers— "twenty-five in all. All in the Moosehead Lake area. At first we thought it was a bunch of isolated incidents. But these birds are picking their places. The break-ins have netted them lots of color televisions, VCRs, those tiny satellite dishes. The estimated value so far is around ten grand. I want you on it and I'd like you to start immediately."

Miki felt as though she were in twin universes—the woman who wanted to be with Christina was in one, and the woman who wanted to be a colonel was in the other. She had to choose one, or lose both.

"Would it be possible, sir, for Charlie Blackman to handle it?"

As she spoke, Miki realized that for the first time in her career, she had put her personal life before her job. Now that the words were out, she felt relief. She had been a fool. She was in love, but

150

she had been too cowardly to admit it even to herself. Now she realized that her dream of being head of the warden service had been lost in the hot glow of Christina.

"Reason?"

"Well, I'm not quite as confident as Peter is that everything has been resolved down there."

"Explain?"

"I think more than one person is involved." Faced with a choice about the future, Miki knew she had to get back to Christina. She realized she felt empty away from Christina. Somehow they had developed a bond, something she had never felt with any other woman.

"Can you be more specific?"

"Nothing tangible at this point."

"Have there been any more harassment problems?"

"No, sir."

"Has an agreement been reached with the lake users over access?"

"Yes, sir."

"Then what am I not seeing here?" The colonel leaned back in his chair. He steepled his outstretched fingers and waited.

"I think someone may have put Billy Clark up to what he did. I don't have any proof, but I'd sure like to go back and get some."

"Have you discussed this with the sheriff?"

"No, sir."

The colonel frowned. "One of the things—" The colonel paused deliberately. "Peter complained to me that several times you left him out of the loop. He said you were a one-woman police force. Now, I understand that. I've done it myself. I prefer to work a case myself instead of dragging in the locals, many of whom are absolutely incompetent. But you offended people there. Was there any reason why you couldn't discuss this with Peter?"

Miki knew she didn't have hard proof of Scott's involvement. Sure, he might have been playing around in her case, but that hardly made him an accessory. "It's just that I hoped to wind this case up myself. As you say, sir, sometimes its better to work a case alone."

"I'm going to need something more than that to hang my decision on."

"Well, take the defendant, Billy Clark. He's not the sharpest knife in the drawer. I think someone put him up to it, just to scare Christina, ah, Mrs. Reynolds." Miki flushed as she corrected herself. "It got out of hand when Clark saw the woman, and I think he decided to do more."

"I understand from Peter she is quite beautiful."

Miki stopped, surprised at the instant flash of jealousy she felt. "She is an attractive woman, yes, sir." Miki forced herself not to focus on the past weekend.

The colonel, astute and incisive in his interviewing skills, watched her. Miki did not discount his investigative techniques. Although his questions seemed simplistic, she knew he could read a subject better than a psychologist.

"I'd like to go back and see if I can wind up this case. At this point, sir, I don't feel it is finished." Miki's stare was unwavering.

"And if I deny your request?"

"I'd like to put in for my two weeks' vacation."

"You feel that strongly."

"Yes, sir, I feel that strongly."

The colonel tilted back in his chair. "Interesting. You've never done this before."

"No, sir." Miki sat very still, determined to match his stare.

The colonel blinked first. "I'll give you another two weeks. If you have nothing, you're back here. Understood? No compromise, and any request for vacation time will be denied."

"Yes, sir."

Miki didn't bother to check the messages on her desk. She called Christina from her office and was upset when there was no answer. An uneasiness settled over her. It was a new feeling, one she didn't know how to handle. She had a bundle of problems that had to be sorted out, and Christina was at the center. Miki pushed her ranger's hat back on her head as she settled behind the wheel of her truck. What made this most difficult was that she had no frame of reference for this new feeling.

Déjà vu, Miki thought as the night came on. She turned on her lights and windshield wipers as she drove into a coastal storm. Two months ago she had been on her way to Bailey's Cove wondering what she was going to do to solve some city woman's problems. Those problems now seemed small compared to the lifetime solutions she knew Christina was wondering about.

For the first time, Miki understood what it meant to be in love. There had been other women in her life, but no one had touched her with such intensity. She knew she wanted to make a lifetime commitment. But she also knew there were huge snowdrifts of problems ahead. If she had been a ranger in California or Massachusetts, it would have been a lot easier, but in Maine there was little room for tolerance. She was in a man's profession, and once they learned she lived with another woman, any acceptance she may have earned would end. She now knew that if she wanted to remain a ranger she was going to have to be the pioneer, breaking new ground. She turned the fan up on the heater. One more hour and she'd be home.

Miki sighed, because even as she realized that she could accept this new career challenge, she also knew there were other problems. She was aspen and hackmatack trees, campfires and canoes. Christina was Neiman Marcus and Tiffany's, marble fireplaces and yachts. Once the heat of passion wore off, would Christina want to settle into life with a ranger? Miki ran this morning, afraid to confront these thoughts. But now the loneliness she had felt these last few hours were unendurable. For Miki, there could be no future without Christina.

She drove directly to Christina's house, and when she didn't find her at home, she sat in her truck and waited. She turned on

153

the overhead light. It was six. She started the engine on her truck. Maybe Christina had left a message on her answering machine. Back at her cabin she picked up an armful of logs and carried them inside. The message machine was silent.

Frustrated, she picked up her telephone to make certain there was a dial tone. Miki dumped the logs near the stove and paced, then picked up the telephone again and dialed Kristan's office. After four rings she got the answering machine and hung up. She called Christina's number again and listened to a ringing telephone.

Miki looked at her watch, six-thirty. Calm down, she told that anxious side of her personality that did not deal well with this kind of tension. How arrogant, she thought. Had she expected Christina to sit and wait until she sorted through her feelings? "Serves you right Miki Jamieson, if the woman went back to Boston," she said aloud, kicking over a chair. She would make one more call and then go back to Christina's house and camp out.

Jennifer picked up on the second ring, and Miki frowned, saying, "I know, I should have returned Kristan's calls. I'm sorry. I haven't been very attentive to details lately."

"No argument here."

"I—I was wondering if you've by chance heard from Christina?"

"Christina?" Jennifer said, her tone a little too coy for Miki's liking.

"I called her house and there was no answer. I was thinking of going over there and waiting. She might be in town."

"Where are you?"

"At my cabin."

"Your cabin. Why don't you come over here, have some supper?"

"Thanks, another time. I really need to talk to her. I left this morning and—"

"Hi." Christina's voice was gentle.

Miki gripped the side of the table. "I—I."

"I'm leaving now. I can be at your cabin in fifteen minutes."

Miki dumped another armload of wood into the stove. She paced nervously back and forth. She tried to stay focused on what she wanted to say to Christina. She walked to the door, opened it and looked outside for the twenty-fifth time. She picked up the telephone listening for a dial tone, afraid Christina might have had a problem on the road and needed to call her. She adjusted the shade on her lamp.

You've got to tell her, she told herself. You've got to say the words. But what if she doesn't love you? What if, what if, what if? She sat down in the chair. Then bounced back up again and began to pace. "Shower," she said aloud. "I need a shower."

Miki saw the lights in the driveway before she heard the engine. She opened the door and ran outside. The door on the Mercedes was opening before it stopped. Miki reached for Christina and pulled her against her. Her mouth was hungry, her arms demanding.

"I love you, I love you," Miki said in between kisses. She buried her face against Christina's neck, the fur collar on Christina's coat soft against her face. "Please say you love me."

Christina reached up to Miki's face and looked deeply in her eyes. "More than life itself."

Miki kissed her eyes and tasted the tears on her eyelashes. She took Christina's hand and led her into the cabin.

Just inside the door they kissed long and deep. The emotions Miki had felt on the drive back from Jackman burst like water through a broken dam. "I want to talk," she said in between kisses.

"I want to make love with you," Christina said shyly. "I want you." She began to unbutton Miki's shirt. She boldly slid the shirt down over Miki's arms, the buttons on the cuffs holding her wrists inside the shirt. She lifted Miki's T-shirt and kissed her again, her tongue drawing circles around her navel. She lifted the shirt even higher and kissed her breasts, moving from one to the other nipple. Miki groaned and felt her knees give way. "I want to touch you everywhere," Christina said against Miki's breasts. She opened Miki's pants, then kissed her belly, her tongue slowly following the opening zipper.

Miki let Christina undress her. "You learn fast," she murmured.

"Umm. I had a great teacher." Christina said with lion-hearted confidence.

Miki willed herself to go slowly as she undressed Christina. Then she lay on the bed and pulled Christina on top of her. "Make love to me," she whispered.

Later, Christina lay curled against Miki's side. "You really believe Scott is somehow involved?"

"Somehow."

"How?"

"I don't think he paid him to harass you, but I think he might have encouraged it. When it escalated, he didn't know how to get out of it without exposing his part."

"But why?"

"That part I don't know, but I can guess."

Christina raised up on her elbow. With her index finger she followed the outline of Miki's ear. "You have the most enchanting ear. I never really looked at an ear before."

"Everything about you is enchanting." Miki kissed Christina's palm.

"You keep doing that, and we're not going to finish talking."

"Well," Miki said as she rolled on top of Christina, "the bad guys are not going anywhere. You have a spot right here that I love." Miki kissed Christina's shoulder. "A little dimple right here." She let her tongue trail over the spot she had just kissed. Christina shivered. "That's the spot, and it always brings a shiver." Miki kissed it again. "Kristan says I'm a jerk because I was afraid to tell you how I felt."

"You're not a—"

"Let me finish," Miki said gently. "She was right." The words helped affirm the emotions she'd felt during her drive to Jackman.

"When I left yesterday morning, I was running away from the responsibility of falling in love. I figured we'd have a weekend here and there. But when I came back and found you gone, I got . . . scared. Scared that you had gone back to Boston." Miki struggled with the words. "I didn't know where you were and I nearly went crazy. I don't want life to be like that. I want to own that part of your life that makes you mine. Not in the sense of total possession, but in the sense that you want me to know where you are. You want to tell me what you're doing and what you're thinking." Miki kissed Christina on the forehead. "I want to feel secure that someone also worries about me. Thinks about me." Miki laughed, embarrassed at herself. "But now I'm holding my breath because I don't know what you want."

Christina had been quiet. "I knew the moment we danced and you held me"—Christina touched Miki's arms— "this was where I wanted to be" Christina leaned back and looked in her eyes. "That night I confronted what I didn't want to confront before I fell in love with you." She grinned impishly. "I never saw anyone look like you did that night. You were praying the earth would open up and swallow you whole."

"You're right. I didn't know what to do. I knew what I wanted to do. This . . ." Miki kissed her and held her. "I want you to meet my parents." Miki laughed. "Now that's a first."

"Oh God, I hadn't thought about that part. How will they react?"

"Mother will cry. Dad will just stare."

"Do they know about you?"

"They know. They just don't think about it."

"They're going to hate me."

"No, love, they are going to absolutely adore you. I promise."

Christina leaned up on her elbow. "Now, telling John is going to be something else. I told you John and I had a long talk when I went back there."

"Yes, I wondered about the details, but I guessed the subject matter. You told him what you were feeling?"

"I told him I was attracted to you." Christina averted her eyes and sighed. "Always the pragmatist, he said he viewed it as super dependency, because of the harassment and the scare. Discounted it as that."

"Won't he be surprised."

Miki stroked Christina's cheek. her fingers lingering at the edge of her mouth. "I do know something I want, though."

"What's that?"

"A king-size bed. People shouldn't have to make love in such a small nest."

Miki kissed Christina and felt the heat rise in her. Solutions, they would look for solutions, but not now.

Chapter Eighteen

On Wednesday morning, Miki found herself seated across from Jennifer in her office. "I've increased the pressure. His attorney has asked for a reduced sentence, a plea agreement that would give him thirty days in jail, all suspended."

"What did you tell them?"

"To pound sand. No plea unless it includes some jail time, even a week. Right now he's looking at three to five years. But, Miki, you have to understand there's no way, even if a jury finds him guilty, that he's going to see anything more than probably a few days in jail. I'm just sounding tough, but Bob Carter isn't a fool."

"True, but his client is. I think he's scared. You know he was in a mental institution. Did you find out why?"

"He's a diagnosed manic-depressive with a couple of other personality problems. He attempted suicide, a very self-destructive guy. But I think the most critical piece of information is that he's claustrophobic. No way he wants to go to jail. I think he feels he'll go bonkers."

"The last time I saw him I felt he was close to the edge."

"Edge as in suicide?"

"Edge as in I don't know what he might do." Miki shifted in her seat. "I was coming out of Lincoln's Department Store. He was going in. He saw me and ran in the opposite direction. He's scared, and I think someone is pushing all the right buttons to reinforce that feeling."

"I don't understand." Jennifer sat back in her chair. Her brown hair brushed her shoulders.

"I think someone put him up to this."

"Why didn't you tell me that before? I could have used it to bargain a suspended sentence in exchange for giving up his partner."

"I don't think it's so much a partner as a suggestion that went wrong."

Jennifer waited. "Can you elaborate?"

Miki scratched her head. "Not now. Maybe later. I think if we can get this guy in jail for a while, the rest will go away. At least that's the way I read it."

"So you have a suspect."

"Suspect, yes. Tangible proof? No."

"And you're not going to tell me." Miki heard the irritation in her voice.

"Not because I don't want to. It's just that I've been fishing a lot of lines, with no success. The problem is the colonel told me to stay away from Clark. But I'll tell you one thing, Jennifer, when he turned tail and ran the other day, there was fear in his eyes, clear, naked fear. I saw it."

"I can't force you to tell me, but I think you have to trust me as a friend, let's leave me as a prosecutor out for a moment. But more important, maybe you need to have an outsider look at your evidence."

Miki hesitated. "I could be wrong."

"You could be right, and if that's the case, something should be done about it."

Miki studied the picture behind Jennifer; a Maine seascape with colorful boats and weathered lobster traps. "Okay." She was silent for a long while as she thought about how she would tell Jennifer. "I think Scott had a hand in this."

"Scott? Why?"

"He was assigned to the case. I understand from Christina, he came on to her hard. Asked her out, she declined. Then, when I was ordered to take over the case, everything got really screwy. At first, I thought he was just mucking around in my case. Later, I wasn't so sure. Things got really primal after that. I think he had figured out I had fallen for Christina."

"He'd screw up his career because he's jealous?" Jennifer frowned. "He may be stupid, but that would be crazy."

"Oh, I don't think he put a gun in Billy's hand, but I think he fueled Billy's belief he owned the land. I think he goaded him into scaring Christina. But that night Billy tried to get into Christina's house, I think Scott got scared. I think he talked to him that night at the jail. I think he's the one paying for the expensive attorney. Beyond that, I'm not sure."

"You want me to call Scott in, see what he has to say?"

"Don't do that." Miki was alarmed. She still wasn't sure if Scott was involved. "All I have is conjecture."

"You owe it to Scott to talk to him."

"I know."

"And soon."

"But it could be a moot point if Billy doesn't show."

"You think he might run again?"

"Let's just say I wouldn't be surprised."

"You know there's nothing I can do about that. I can't call his attorney and say I don't think your client is going to show up."

"So what if he doesn't show up? That means he's out of here. Away from Christina."

"That's not very cop-like."

"When it comes to Christina I find myself otherwise."

"How are things?" Jennifer asked softly.

161

"It's like an emotional weightlessness. I'm just floating and damn happy to be doing it." Miki grinned.

"Christina looks happy."

"She is."

"Plans for the future?"

"Well, when this ends we're going to go to Jackman. We'll just take one day at a time after that."

"Miki, I'm glad. I know how you've struggled with this."

"Yeah, and I'm certain I'm going to keep struggling. You know the kind of scumbags I arrest. Instead of calling me a queer behind my back, they do it to my face. I expect slippage and frustration, but I discovered one thing that I never ever included in my frame of reference before."

"What's that?" Jennifer asked, as if on cue.

"Being so much in love that I can't think of living life without her. She already feels a part of me, and no one ever has before."

"Do you think you two can take enough time to have dinner with Kristan and me, say, Thursday night? Give us a chance to talk one last time before court Friday morning."

"You're on. Let me talk it over with Christina, and I'll give you a call." Miki stopped and laughed. "Wow, that feels so strange. Having to check with someone before I make a decision. That is going to take some getting used to."

"You'd be surprised how easy that is, my friend."

Miki stood up. She stepped toward the door and then turned. "Jennifer, thanks."

"She's a keeper, Mik, and I'm glad you found her," Jennifer said sincerely.

On Friday morning, Miki sat next to Jennifer at the district attorney's table. They'd had dinner the night before, and she felt confident about the proceedings.

"Miki, can I see you a minute?" She saw the grim expression on Peter's face. He nodded toward the back of the room.

162

Jennifer looked from Peter to Miki. "You need me there?" she asked Peter.

"Maybe later, right now I need to talk to Miki."

Miki glanced over at Christina who was sitting in the last row. When she smiled Miki felt a stirring deep inside. They had been together every moment since she'd returned from Jackman, and Miki now knew what a junky felt like. The more she was with her, the more she wanted her. "Court's ready to start." Miki said as she looked at her watch.

"We have a few minutes, the court clerk isn't in her seat yet."

Miki watched as Peter struggled with what he wanted to say. "Scott came to my house last night," he blurted out. "I think you probably know what it's about." Miki nodded. "I've suspended him until I can sort this out, but he claims it started out as some kind of rivalry between you two. He said it just got out of hand, and the night Billy showed up at Christina's with the gun, he panicked. He's sure Billy's going to implicate him and say he put him up to it. He swears he had no idea what Billy was going to do."

"What do you want to do?"

"That's the hard part. He wants to resign, but"— Miki could see the anxiety in Peter's eyes— "if he's responsible for Billy doing what he did, Scott has to be prosecuted."

"Let me talk to Mrs. Reynolds"—Miki looked over at Christina— "where's Scott now?"

"I told him to stay home until I contacted him."

The door to the judge's chambers opened. "All rise," bailiff Gerald Canter ordered. "The honorable Justice William McKinnon presiding."

"Let's talk, later," Miki whispered.

"Be seated," the judge told the courtroom. Miki sat down next to Jennifer. She could read the questions in Jennifer's eyes.

He opened a file in front of him. "Docket number 98-128. Is the state ready to proceed?"

"Yes, Your Honor." Jennifer stood and responded to the judge.

"Is the defense ready?"

"No, Your Honor." Carter also was on his feet.

"Is there a problem, Counsel?"

"Well, Your Honor, it appears that my client is late or lost."

The judge did not smile. "When were you last in contact with him?"

"Yesterday, Your Honor. I made him aware that he was to be arraigned today, and he assured me he was ready to enter a plea."

Miki gave Jennifer a startled look. Jennifer shrugged. "No one told me he was going to enter a plea," Jennifer whispered.

The judge looked at Peter. "Why don't you have one of your people check around to make certain he isn't wandering around the courthouse."

Peter whispered to the bailiff standing next to him.

"I should go with him," Miki whispered to Jennifer.

"No, you stay here. I don't want him to wander in and then have to tell the judge that my arresting officer is lost. Be patient. This won't take long."

Miki heard the door to the courtroom open. The bailiff bent down and whispered to the sheriff, "It appears he's not here, Your Honor," Peter said.

"In that case, Your Honor," Jennifer said as she stood to address the judge, "I request a bench warrant."

"Granted. One thousand dollars cash bail." Judge McKinnon wrote on a piece of paper. He looked over at Peter. "Bring him in." The judge stood up.

"Yes, Your Honor."

"All rise," the bailiff intoned.

"Miki, come here." Peter gestured to where he and one of his bailiffs were standing. "I'm going out to Greely Point, see if he's there," Peter zipped up his jacket.

"You want me to go with you?"

"I don't expect any problems. If he's there, I'll bring him in. You might spook him."

Just then, Kristan came in saying she was late because she had been at an interview. Peter nodded to Kristan and left. She looked questioningly at Miki, who shrugged. "He's a no-show."

"Really?" Kristan's eyebrows shot up.

"Peter is going over to see if he's at his cabin. He doesn't know it, but I'm going to follow him. I want to be there in case . . ." She let her words trail off.

"Be careful."

"Slam dunk, pal. His record doesn't show any violent crimes. The time he took the crowbar to me at Christina's house was probably just a fluke." She winked at Kristan and went to where Christina and Jennifer were talking at the rear of the courtroom.

"I'm going to Greely Point to find Clark," she said to Christina.

"Is that smart?" Jennifer asked.

"It could be dangerous." Christina said.

Miki read the fear in her eyes. She resisted the desire to take her in her arms and tell her it would be all right. "It's okay," she said to the two women. "He's not dangerous. I think he's just scared. I'll see you tonight." Miki gave Christina a half-smile.

"Be careful," Jennifer said as she walked back to the counsel table to gather up her files.

"Your place or mine?" Christina asked Miki.

"Mine." Miki noted that Christina returned a smile she clearly did not feel.

"I plan to cook you a huge meal and build up your strength," she whispered. "Please be careful."

"I will. See you tonight." Miki touched the top of Christina's hands and let her fingers linger there for just a moment.

She knew Peter was already out of the courthouse and in his cruiser. Miki ran to her truck. She wasn't as confidant as Peter that he wouldn't need help. She headed toward the woods road that led to Greely Point. She slowed when she came to Billy's driveway, then drove toward the house.

Peter was beside his cruiser. The hood on Billy's beat-up Chevy was up. He must have had car trouble, Miki thought. "Figured you could use some help." Miki said as she stepped out of the truck. She looked at the house. The window shades were drawn, she saw black smoke coming from the chimney.

"Betcha he's here."

"Looks like it." Peter reached for his microphone and switched his radio to loudspeaker. "Mr. Clark, this is Sheriff Peter Kelley of the County Sheriff's Department. I want you to step outside please."

Miki watched the house. "Tell him he should give himself up and no one will get hurt," she said to Peter. Miki waited. If Billy Clark was looking out a window, she wanted him to see that she did not have a gun in her hand. She moved carefully to the front of her truck.

Peter again told Billy to give himself up. "What'd ya think?" he rested his chin on the microphone.

"I don't know. I hate to spook him, but I think we'd better call for backup. Neither one of us wants this to turn nasty."

Peter reached in and switched back to his radio. "I have a ten-seventy-four at Greely Point," he told the dispatcher. "Notify the Maine State Police."

"Ten-four."

"Peter, look at that smoke. It looks as though it's coming from more than just his wood stove." Peter looked to where Miki was pointing. Large puffs of black smoke were coming from the rear of the cabin. "I think the cabin's on fire," she said anxiously.

Peter switched his radio back to loudspeaker. "Billy Clark, this is the sheriff. I want you to step outside with your hands up." Miki watched for any sign of movement near the windows. "Look, no one is going to hurt you."

Miki pointed. "Look, flames." Miki ran toward the cabin when she heard a muffled shot. At the same time she saw flames licking up the wall, catching the window curtains on fire. She crept closer, Peter behind her. She picked up a couple of large rocks and threw them, breaking the window near the door and waited to see if Clark would respond. All she could hear was the crackling sound of burning wood. She crawled up to a window on the front porch and yanked down a curtain that had not yet burned. The smoke was thick. Miki tried to look inside, but the smoke stung her eyes and forced her away from the window. She crouched down, wiping her eyes.

"See anything?" Peter asked.

"Can't tell. The smoke's thick, but I don't see any movement. I think he shot himself and he's cooking in there," Miki said. "Better call the fire department and the medical examiner. I'll see if I can get inside. He could be alive." Miki felt the cabin door, then crouched down again and reached for the handle. She might be able to reach him, she thought, if she crawled in.

"Be careful," Peter warned. He turned toward his car when he heard a crack and then a ripping sound. "Look out!" Miki screamed as the roof crashed down on her, narrowly missing Peter. Miki groaned. She heard Peter yelling and felt the weight of the roof beam being pulled off of her, then she blacked out.

Christina carried a bouquet of roses. Miki was sitting up in a chair when Christina arrived, she gave Miki a lingering kiss.

"How's it feel?" Christina touched the bandaged shoulder with her fingertips. She had been at the hospital every day since Miki was injured. When the roof collapsed, a beam had narrowly missed her head and crashed into her shoulder.

"Better. I'm so glad you're here." Miki touched Christina's face with her good hand. "Thank you." Miki smelled the flowers. "My favorite." She stroked the petals with her fingers. "It's only been a few hours since I've seen you, but I've missed you. I've been negotiating with Jackie about going home."

"When?" Christina took the flowers and put them in water. Miki saw that Christina was distracted.

"Tomorrow. I can't go back to work, and there'll be a lot of physical therapy, but I can do that as an outpatient." Miki paused. "What's wrong?"

"You could have been killed." Christina eyes were a blur of tears. This was an issue they had discussed continuously since Miki was injured. "I had no idea your job was so dangerous. First you're struck by a crowbar, then nearly killed by a falling roof. Am I going to have to sit at home and wonder what the next calamity might be?"

"Absolutely not. You remember that first day we met and you asked me if I had ever shot my gun at anyone? I told you then that there was very little excitement in my job. This has been an unusual few months." Miki held her hand out. "Come here, please," she said softly.

Christina cuddled into Miki's good arm. "I don't want to hurt your shoulder."

"You can't. Christina, I love you, and I promise you this won't ever happen again. We're called tree huggers, and we come by our name honestly. Never, do we see this much action." Miki stroked her hair.

Christina jumped when she heard the rap on the hospital door. She quickly pushed her hand through her hair. "Come in." Miki grinned.

"Hi, Christina. Hey, Miki, how ya doing?" Peter handed her a box of candy. "The wife sent these." He seemed almost embarrassed about the gift.

"Thank you," Miki suppressed a grin. Peter's sudden appearance had Christina unnerved. She looked like the child caught sneaking her mother's makeup. "Sit down Peter."

"Thank you. I'm glad you're here, Christina. I've spent quite a bit of time with Scott these past few days. We've talked a lot about the attempted break-in at your house, and I think he's ready to own up to his role in it. I told him I plan to charge him as an accessory to the crime."

Christina looked over at Miki. "Peter, I don't want Scott charged. I've been thinking a lot about this too, and"—she paused— "I feel terrible that a man is dead, and I really don't want this to go any further. Doing something to Scott is not going to make any of this right."

"Christina, Billy's death had nothing to do with you," Miki frowned. They had not talked about Scott's being charged, and she was at a loss to figure out where Christina was going with this. "Billy Clark could have hurt you if he'd gotten into the house, and when he did that he thought he had Scott's backing. I really can't forgive that," Miki said.

"Scott admits he crossed the line," Peter joined in. "Oh, he denies he told Billy to break into your house, but he admits that he encouraged him to harass you. It was all very weird. He had this crazy idea that if you got rattled enough, you'd turn to him for"— Peter stood up and stared out the window— "I had no idea he was as upset as he was being taken off the case. I guess I should have . . ." Peter stopped.

Miki reached up and touched her bandaged shoulder. She had to stop thinking like a cop, she thought. She looked at Peter, "If Christina doesn't want Scott charged, then I think we have to honor her decision." Miki read the relief in Christina's eyes. "But I don't want him around here."

"Actually, he's already said he wants to leave. I expect now that he's not going to be charged, he'll move back to Connecticut," Peter sat back down.

"I—" Christina stopped. "Any idea why Billy killed himself?"

Peter stared at the tiles on the ceiling and then looked at Christina. "I talked with Jennifer. She's finally gotten hold of all of his records. Seems he's been in and out of mental hospitals for quite some time now. Manic-depression, panic attacks and serious claustrophobia. There were even two attempts at suicide. One of them while he was in jail on a minor misdemeanor charge." Peter shook his head as he recalled the list Jennifer had read to him.

"I think Billy felt boxed in," Miki said reflectively as the single gunshot echoed in her memory. "I think he started to leave but couldn't get his car started. When we showed up, he couldn't face going back to jail. In some ways"—she looked over at Peter—"I'm just as responsible for Billy's death as anyone. I bullied him."

Miki saw Christina's frown. She recounted her visit to his cabin and the panic she saw in his eyes.

"Let's not play the blame game," Peter said quietly. "Billy's dead because he pulled the trigger. And no amount of hand wringing or blame is going to bring us any closer to why he did it. It happened. It's bad, but it happened." He repeated himself. Peter stood up. "Look, I've got to get back to the office." He reached out his hand to Christina. "Thank you. I'll tell Scott what you said. And thank you, Miki. Stop by the office when you get back on your feet."

Christina followed him and quietly closed the door. "I feel terrible," she said as she turned back to Miki. Miki pulled her against her and gently kissed her lips. Christina kissed Miki's neck. "I love you so much, but I'll tell you this, Miki Jamieson, if you ever get hurt like this again, I'll kill you." For the first time in days a smile played across Christina's lips.

"It has been a busy morning," Miki eased herself back into her chair. "The colonel visited me earlier today."

"Good, bad, what?" Christina placed her hand on Miki's knee.

"Between asking when I could go back to work and telling me to take as much time as I need, he told me he was relieved that I wasn't killed." Miki laughed. "I told him the doctors said I'd only be down for a couple of weeks." Miki put her fingers under Christina's chin and looked into her eyes. "I also told him that although my career was important to me, I was going to be more focused on my personal life from now on."

"What did he say?"

"He didn't seem surprised. He's a damn good cop. I wouldn't be surprised if he knew I'm involved with you, probably heard it from Peter. I couldn't really tell if he cared or not."

"But do you care what he thinks?"

Miki paused, "Not now." Miki pulled Christina tightly against her, "I just want to go home. I've missed you. I want to make love to you," she said softly.

Christina looked at Miki's heavily bandaged right shoulder. "With one wing? I think not."

Miki kissed her deeply. "I've been thinking of some creative ways to get around my shoulder," she grinned. "Lock the door."

FOR EVERY SEASON by Frankie Jones. 240 pp. Andi, who is investigating a 65-year-old murder, meets Janice, a charming district attorney . . . ISBN 1-59493-010-4 $12.95

LOVE ON THE LINE by Laura DeHart Young. 240 pp. Kay leaves a younger woman behind to go on a mission to Alaska . . . will she regret it? ISBN 1-59493-008-2 $12.95

UNDER THE SOUTHERN CROSS by Claire McNab. 200 pp. Lee, an American travel agent, goes down under and meets Australian Alex, and the sparks fly under the Southern Cross. ISBN 1-59493-029-5 $12.95

SUGAR by Karin Kallmaker. 240 pp. Three women want sugar from Sugar, who can't make up her mind. ISBN 1-59493-001-5 $12.95

FALL GUY by Claire McNab. 200 pp. 16th Detective Inspector Carol Ashton Mystery. ISBN 1-59493-000-7 $12.95

ONE SUMMER NIGHT by Gerri Hill. 232 pp. Johanna swore to never fall in love again— but then she met the charming Kelly . . . ISBN 1-59493-007-4 $12.95

TALK OF THE TOWN TOO by Saxon Bennett. 181 pp. Second in the series about wild and fun loving friends. ISBN 1-931513-77-5 $12.95

LOVE SPEAKS HER NAME by Laura DeHart Young. 170 pp. Love and friendship, desire and intrigue, spark this exciting sequel to *Forever and the Night*. ISBN 1-59493-002-3 $12.95

TO HAVE AND TO HOLD by Peggy J. Herring. 184 pp. By finally letting down her defenses, will Dorian be opening herself to a devastating betrayal? ISBN 1-59493-005-8 $12.95

WILD THINGS by Karin Kallmaker. 228 pp. Dutiful daughter Faith has met the perfect man. There's just one problem: she's in love with his sister. ISBN 1-931513-64-3 $12.95

SHARED WINDS by Kenna White. 216 pp. Can Emma rebuild more than just Lanny's marina? ISBN 1-59493-006-6 $12.95

THE UNKNOWN MILE by Jaime Clevenger. 253 pp. Kelly's world is getting more and more complicated every moment. ISBN 1-931513-57-0 $12.95

TREASURED PAST by Linda Hill. 189 pp. A shared passion for antiques leads to love. ISBN 1-59493-003-1 $12.95

SIERRA CITY by Gerri Hill. 284 pp. Chris and Jesse cannot deny their growing attraction . . . ISBN 1-931513-98-8 $12.95

ALL THE WRONG PLACES by Karin Kallmaker. 174 pp. Sex and the single girl—Brandy is looking for love and usually she finds it. Karin Kallmaker's first *After Dark* erotic novel. ISBN 1-931513-76-7 $12.95

WHEN THE CORPSE LIES A Motor City Thriller by Therese Szymanski. 328 pp. Butch bad-girl Brett Higgins is used to waking up next to beautiful women she hardly knows. Problem is, this one's dead. ISBN 1-931513-74-0 $12.95

GUARDED HEARTS by Hannah Rickard. 240 pp. Someone's reminding Alyssa about her secret past, and then she becomes the suspect in a series of burglaries. ISBN 1-931513-99-6 $12.95

ONCE MORE WITH FEELING by Peggy J. Herring. 184 pp. Lighthearted, loving, romantic adventure. ISBN 1-931513-60-0 $12.95

TANGLED AND DARK A Brenda Strange Mystery by Patty G. Henderson. 240 pp. When investigating a local death, Brenda finds two possible killers—one diagnosed with Multiple Personality Disorder. ISBN 1-931513-75-9 $12.95

WHITE LACE AND PROMISES by Peggy J. Herring. 240 pp. Maxine and Betina realize sex may not be the most important thing in their lives. ISBN 1-931513-73-2 $12.95

UNFORGETTABLE by Karin Kallmaker. 288 pp. Can Rett find love with the cheerleader who broke her heart so many years ago? ISBN 1-931513-63-5 $12.95

HIGHER GROUND by Saxon Bennett. 280 pp. A delightfully complex reflection of the successful, high society lives of a small group of women. ISBN 1-931513-69-4 $12.95

LAST CALL A Detective Franco Mystery by Baxter Clare. 240 pp. Frank overlooks all else to try to solve a cold case of two murdered children . . . ISBN 1-931513-70-8 $12.95

ONCE UPON A DYKE: NEW EXPLOITS OF FAIRY-TALE LESBIANS by Karin Kallmaker, Julia Watts, Barbara Johnson & Therese Szymanski. 320 pp. You've never read fairy tales like these before! From Bella After Dark. ISBN 1-931513-71-6 $14.95

FINEST KIND OF LOVE by Diana Tremain Braund. 224 pp. Can Molly and Carolyn stop clashing long enough to see beyond their differences? ISBN 1-931513-68-6 $12.95

DREAM LOVER by Lyn Denison. 188 pp. A soft, sensuous, romantic fantasy.
ISBN 1-931513-96-1 $12.95

NEVER SAY NEVER by Linda Hill. 224 pp. A classic love story . . . where rules aren't the only things broken. ISBN 1-931513-67-8 $12.95

PAINTED MOON by Karin Kallmaker. 214 pp. Stranded together in a snowbound cabin, Jackie and Leah's lives will never be the same. ISBN 1-931513-53-8 $12.95

WIZARD OF ISIS by Jean Stewart. 240 pp. Fifth in the exciting Isis series.
ISBN 1-931513-71-4 $12.95

WOMAN IN THE MIRROR by Jackie Calhoun. 216 pp. Josey learns to love again, while her niece is learning to love women for the first time. ISBN 1-931513-78-3 $12.95

SUBSTITUTE FOR LOVE by Karin Kallmaker. 200 pp. When Holly and Reyna meet the combination adds up to pure passion. But what about tomorrow? ISBN 1-931513-62-7 $12.95

GULF BREEZE by Gerri Hill. 288 pp. Could Carly really be the woman Pat has always been searching for? ISBN 1-931513-97-X $12.95

THE TOMSTOWN INCIDENT by Penny Hayes. 184 pp. Caught between two worlds, Eloise must make a decision that will change her life forever. ISBN 1-931513-56-2 $12.95

MAKING UP FOR LOST TIME by Karin Kallmaker. 240 pp. Discover delicious recipes for romance by the undisputed mistress. ISBN 1-931513-61-9 $12.95

THE WAY LIFE SHOULD BE by Diana Tremain Braund. 173 pp. With which woman will Jennifer find the true meaning of love? ISBN 1-931513-66-X $12.95

BACK TO BASICS: A BUTCH/FEMME ANTHOLOGY edited by Therese Szymanski—from Bella After Dark. 324 pp. ISBN 1-931513-35-X $14.95

SURVIVAL OF LOVE by Frankie J. Jones. 236 pp. What will Jody do when she falls in love with her best friend's daughter? ISBN 1-931513-55-4 $12.95

LESSONS IN MURDER by Claire McNab. 184 pp. 1st Detective Inspector Carol Ashton Mystery. ISBN 1-931513-65-1 $12.95

DEATH BY DEATH by Claire McNab. 167 pp. 5th Denise Cleever Thriller.
ISBN 1-931513-34-1 $12.95

CAUGHT IN THE NET by Jessica Thomas. 188 pp. A wickedly observant story of mystery, danger, and love in Provincetown.
ISBN 1-931513-54-6 $12.95

DREAMS FOUND by Lyn Denison. Australian Riley embarks on a journey to meet her birth mother . . . and gains not just a family, but the love of her life.   ISBN 1-931513-58-9 $12.95

A MOMENT'S INDISCRETION by Peggy J. Herring. 154 pp. Jackie is torn between her better judgment and the overwhelming attraction she feels for Valerie.
ISBN 1-931513-59-7 $12.95

IN EVERY PORT by Karin Kallmaker. 224 pp. Jessica has a woman in every port. Will meeting Cat change all that?   ISBN 1-931513-36-8 $12.95

TOUCHWOOD by Karin Kallmaker. 240 pp. Rayann loves Louisa. Louisa loves Rayann. Can the decades between their ages keep them apart?   ISBN 1-931513-37-6 $12.95

WATERMARK by Karin Kallmaker. 248 pp. Teresa wants a future with a woman whose heart has been frozen by loss. Sequel to *Touchwood*.   ISBN 1-931513-38-4 $12.95

EMBRACE IN MOTION by Karin Kallmaker. 240 pp. Has Sarah found lust or love?
ISBN 1-931513-39-2 $12.95

ONE DEGREE OF SEPARATION by Karin Kallmaker. 232 pp. Sizzling small town romance between Marian, the town librarian, and the new girl from the big city.
ISBN 1-931513-30-9 $12.95

CRY HAVOC A Detective Franco Mystery by Baxter Clare. 240 pp. A dead hustler with a headless rooster in his lap sends Lt. L.A. Franco headfirst against Mother Love.
ISBN 1-931513931-7 $12.95

DISTANT THUNDER by Peggy J. Herring. 294 pp. Bankrobbing drifter Cordy awakens strange new feelings in Leo in this romantic tale set in the Old West.
ISBN 1-931513-28-7 $12.95

COP OUT by Claire McNab. 216 pp. 4th Detective Inspector Carol Ashton Mystery.
ISBN 1-931513-29-5 $12.95

BLOOD LINK by Claire McNab. 159 pp. 15th Detective Inspector Carol Ashton Mystery. Is Carol unwittingly playing into a deadly plan?   ISBN 1-931513-27-9 $12.95

TALK OF THE TOWN by Saxon Bennett. 239 pp. With enough beer, barbecue and B.S., anything is possible!   ISBN 1-931513-18-X $12.95

MAYBE NEXT TIME by Karin Kallmaker. 256 pp. Sabrina has everything she ever wanted—except Jorie.   ISBN 1-931513-26-0 $12.95

WHEN GOOD GIRLS GO BAD: A Motor City Thriller by Therese Szymanski. 230 pp. Brett, Randi, and Allie join forces to stop a serial killer.   ISBN 1-931513-11-2 $12.95

A DAY TOO LONG: A Helen Black Mystery by Pat Welch. 328 pp. This time Helen's fate is in her own hands.   ISBN 1-931513-22-8 $12.95

THE RED LINE OF YARMALD by Diana Rivers. 256 pp. The Hadra's only hope lies in a magical red line . . . climactic sequel to *Clouds of War*.   ISBN 1-931513-23-6 $12.95

OUTSIDE THE FLOCK by Jackie Calhoun. 224 pp. Jo embraces her new love and life.
ISBN 1-931513-13-9 $12.95

LEGACY OF LOVE by Marianne K. Martin. 224 pp. Read the whole Sage Bristo story.
ISBN 1-931513-15-5 $12.95

STREET RULES: A Detective Franco Mystery by Baxter Clare. 304 pp. Gritty, fast-paced mystery with compelling Detective L.A. Franco. ISBN 1-931513-14-7 $12.95

RECOGNITION FACTOR: 4th Denise Cleever Thriller by Claire McNab. 176 pp. Denise Cleever tracks a notorious terrorist to America. ISBN 1-931513-24-4 $12.95

NORA AND LIZ by Nancy Garden. 296 pp. Lesbian romance by the author of *Annie on My Mind*. ISBN 1931513-20-1 $12.95

MIDAS TOUCH by Frankie J. Jones. 208 pp. Sandra had everything but love.
ISBN 1-931513-21-X $12.95

BEYOND ALL REASON by Peggy J. Herring. 240 pp. A romance hotter than Texas.
ISBN 1-9513-25-2 $12.95

ACCIDENTAL MURDER: 14th Detective Inspector Carol Ashton Mystery by Claire McNab. 208 pp. Carol Ashton tracks an elusive killer. ISBN 1-931513-16-3 $12.95

SEEDS OF FIRE: Tunnel of Light Trilogy, Book 2 by Karin Kallmaker writing as Laura Adams. 274 pp. In Autumn's dreams no one is who they seem. ISBN 1-931513-19-8 $12.95

DRIFTING AT THE BOTTOM OF THE WORLD by Auden Bailey. 288 pp. Beautifully written first novel set in Antarctica. ISBN 1-931513-17-1 $12.95

CLOUDS OF WAR by Diana Rivers. 288 pp. Women unite to defend Zelindar!
ISBN 1-931513-12-0 $12.95

DEATHS OF JOCASTA: 2nd Micky Knight Mystery by J.M. Redmann. 408 pp. Sexy and intriguing Lambda Literary Award–nominated mystery. ISBN 1-931513-10-4 $12.95

LOVE IN THE BALANCE by Marianne K. Martin. 256 pp. The classic lesbian love story, back in print! ISBN 1-931513-08-2 $12.95

THE COMFORT OF STRANGERS by Peggy J. Herring. 272 pp. Lela's work was her passion . . . until now. ISBN 1-931513-09-0 $12.95

WHEN EVIL CHANGES FACE: A Motor City Thriller by Therese Szymanski. 240 pp. Brett Higgins is back in another heart-pounding thriller. ISBN 0-9677753-3-7 $11.95

CHICKEN by Paula Martinac. 208 pp. Lynn finds that the only thing harder than being in a lesbian relationship is ending one. ISBN 1-931513-07-4 $11.95

TAMARACK CREEK by Jackie Calhoun. 208 pp. An intriguing story of love and danger.
ISBN 1-931513-06-6 $11.95

DEATH BY THE RIVERSIDE: 1st Micky Knight Mystery by J.M. Redmann. 320 pp. Finally back in print, the book that launched the Lambda Literary Award–winning Micky Knight mystery series. ISBN 1-931513-05-8 $11.95

EIGHTH DAY: A Cassidy James Mystery by Kate Calloway. 272 pp. In the eighth install-ment of the Cassidy James mystery series, Cassidy goes undercover at a camp for troubled teens. ISBN 1-931513-04-X $11.95

MIRRORS by Marianne K. Martin. 208 pp. Jean Carson and Shayna Bradley fight for a future together. ISBN 1-931513-02-3 $11.95

THE ULTIMATE EXIT STRATEGY: A Virginia Kelly Mystery by Nikki Baker. 240 pp. The long-awaited return of the wickedly observant Virginia Kelly.
ISBN 1-931513-03-1 $11.95

FOREVER AND THE NIGHT by Laura DeHart Young. 224 pp. Desire and passion ignite the frozen Arctic in this exciting sequel to the classic romantic adventure *Love on the Line*.
ISBN 0-931513-00-7 $11.95

WINGED ISIS by Jean Stewart. 240 pp. The long-awaited sequel to *Warriors of Isis* and the fourth in the exciting Isis series.   ISBN 1-931513-01-5 $11.95

ROOM FOR LOVE by Frankie J. Jones. 192 pp. Jo and Beth must overcome the past in order to have a future together.   ISBN 0-9677753-9-6 $11.95

THE QUESTION OF SABOTAGE by Bonnie J. Morris. 144 pp. A charming, sexy tale of romance, intrigue, and coming of age.   ISBN 0-9677753-8-8 $11.95

SLEIGHT OF HAND by Karin Kallmaker writing as Laura Adams. 256 pp. A journey of passion, heartbreak, and triumph that reunites two women for a final chance at their destiny.   ISBN 0-9677753-7-X $11.95

MOVING TARGETS: A Helen Black Mystery by Pat Welch. 240 pp. Helen must decide if getting to the bottom of a mystery is worth hitting bottom.   ISBN 0-9677753-6-1 $11.95

CALM BEFORE THE STORM by Peggy J. Herring. 208 pp. Colonel Robicheaux retires from the military and comes out of the closet.   ISBN 0-9677753-1-0 $11.95

OFF SEASON by Jackie Calhoun. 208 pp. Pam threatens Jenny and Rita's fledgling relationship.   ISBN 0-9677753-0-2 $11.95

BOLD COAST LOVE by Diana Tremain Braund. 208 pp. Jackie Claymont fights for her reputation and the right to love the woman she chooses.   ISBN 0-9677753-2-9 $11.95

THE WILD ONE by Lyn Denison. 176 pp. Rachel never expected that Quinn's wild yearnings would change her life forever.   ISBN 0-9677753-4-5 $11.95

SWEET FIRE by Saxon Bennett. 224 pp. Welcome to Heroy—the town with more lesbians per capita than any other place on the planet!   ISBN 0-9677753-5-3 $11.95

Visit

Bella Books

at

BellaBooks.com

or call our toll-free number

1-800-729-4992